To Lillie,

The Secret of Hoke Farm

by

Ashlen Brown

Ashln B
2019

TELEMACHUS PRESS

THE SECRET OF HOKE FARM

Cover designed by Telemachus Press, LLC

Cover art by Paul Manfre

Published by Telemachus Press, LLC
http://www.telemachuspress.com

Visit the author website:
http://www.ashlenbrown.com

ISBN: 978-1-941536-61-2 (eBook)
ISBN: 978-1-941536-62-9 (Paperback)

Version 2014.11.18

Printed in the United States of America

10 9 8 7 6 5 4 3 2 1

For my grandmothers, both of whom gave me love and support that will forever inspire me.

CONTENTS

The Secret of Hoke Farm

CHAPTER ONE
The Plan

THE SUN WAS beginning to shine through the thick trees above the tent. It was bathing patches of the shelter in its warmth, sufficiently warming the occupant until he was uncomfortable enough to awaken from his deep sleep. Jim Thomas woke up feeling groggy. He couldn't remember where he was—everything was different. Looking around, he remembered that he was outside, in his tent. He and his friend Charlie had hiked through the twenty-one acres of woods that Jim's family lived in and found a fun place to camp out. It was near the tree fort they had built the summer before.

Since Jim had been given the tent for his thirteenth birthday the week before, he had chosen to sleep in it rather than the fort, and it had been fun. Jim and Charlie had worked at putting it together yesterday afternoon, and it had taken them no time. Charlie had wanted to sleep outside last night, so Jim had the tent all to himself.

Stretching his arms over his head, Jim took in a deep breath. He liked the way the outdoors smelled. Of course, it was mixed with the scent of new tent, but he could still smell the dewy morning. He crawled forward and unzipped the tent door. Poking his head out, he looked at Charlie, who was still asleep. Charlie's massive body was on its right side with his back toward the tent.

Jim smiled. He loved Charlie like a brother.

The thing about Charlie was that he wasn't like anyone else Jim had ever encountered. He was, in fact, a bigfoot. The summer previously, Jim had discovered Charlie, and they had quickly become friends. For a short time, he had kept Charlie all to himself, but his family had quickly learned about his existence. Jim's now nine-year-old sister, Jilly, had taken to him immediately, but his parents had been more hesitant. Once they had seen the kindness in Charlie, they had taken him under their wings like one of their own. Those first few weeks, Charlie and the family had faced danger, but they had stuck together and finally had come out okay, with only a few scary moments—one in particular.

Jim was thinking about the moment when he had thought that he had lost Charlie. It was the worst moment of his life. Since then, Jim had felt like the luckiest guy in the world. He had been loving every minute of life with Charlie.

"Hey! Wake up!" he yelled.

Charlie made a snorting sound and slowly rolled to a sitting position. He looked at Jim and waved sleepily.

Jim laughed at Charlie's sleepy look—thick hair poking up in different directions—and started gathering things to take back to the house. They were going to eat breakfast with Jilly since she hadn't wanted to camp with them. They had planned the camp-out a couple of weeks before when there was a freak cool front that had significantly cooled everything down. But that had come and gone, and heat had replaced it. Jilly had said that she didn't like waking up feeling sticky from the Texas humidity.

Jim thought she had a point. This summer had quickly become unusually hot and humid, even though it had just begun. But it was still amazing. He wouldn't want to be anywhere else.

Looking around, he took in the scenery of the forest. The trees were thick and lush with dark green leaves. There were birds hopping and flying all over the place, squirrels skittering about, and bugs of all kinds flitting here and there.

"Come on, let's get some food," he told Charlie.

Charlie heard the word "food" and perked up. He smiled and started off toward the house with long strides that Jim couldn't hope to match. Charlie was growing. He had been around six feet tall when Jim had met him one year ago, but he was a young bigfoot and he was still growing. Jim knew that he could grow to around seven feet tall because Charlie had shown him how tall his father and brother had been.

While Charlie couldn't speak more than a few small words, he could understand much of what the Thomas family said these days. He was extremely smart and learned very quickly. He communicated very well through drawing pictures, and that was how Jim knew about Charlie's family.

Apparently, Charlie had an older brother and a younger sister. His parents had died, but Jim hadn't yet been able to ask Charlie how. He just couldn't bring himself to do it. However, he knew that a wildfire had forced Charlie and his siblings to flee from their home and had ultimately split them up somehow.

Jim was working on finding out where Charlie had come from exactly, but he was having a hard time explaining the map to Charlie. That was Jim's summer project.

That and to have fun.

As they walked back to the house, Jim was staring at Charlie's huge back. It was covered in long, reddish-brown hair that glinted in the sun. He was thinking about how Charlie had quickly become such an important part of the family.

Over the holidays, Charlie had sat down to his first Thanksgiving dinner. He had tasted all of the foods with enthusiasm, and Jilly had helped him cut his turkey. When they first met

Charlie, they had thought that he was a vegetarian, but they found that he ate certain meats. He was very familiar with fish, but he had taken quickly to eating different meats they provided. The problem was in the cooking. It was very foreign to Charlie and apparently took some getting used to.

Jim had been doing a lot of research. Shortly after they first met, Charlie had learned to say a very crude version of his name. He could say crude versions of a few words but not very well and not all words. It reminded Jim of the way parrots talk. Jim's aunt had a large macaw that could speak certain words but not very clearly. She could mimic certain sounds but not others. For some reason, Charlie worked the same way, but Jim wanted to know why.

The best Jim could do was research why chimps and apes can't speak. He had found that they were not physically built to perform the complex vocalizations that humans were equipped to perform. He had also found a complicated article about a FOXP2 gene that is different in humans. It was too complex for Jim, but from what he could gather, this gene was present in other animals, but they produced different effects at different times in the development of humans in order to give humans the physical and mental capabilities of speech. Jim wasn't sure where Charlie stood on the evolutionary time line, but he figured that Charlie didn't have the same copies of this gene or that they were functional at different times than in human development. All he really knew was that Charlie was more like a parrot than a person when it came to speech. However, he could understand a whole lot more.

That was fine with him. Jim didn't need speech from Charlie. He loved him anyway.

One thing that Jim and his family had noticed in more recent days was that Charlie spent his nights staring off in the distance and seemed lost in thought. Jim saw sadness in his eyes at these times and knew that Charlie was thinking of his family. If there was one thing Jim wanted for Charlie, it was to find out what had happened to his family.

They walked through the thick brush of the Texas woods and wound along the trail that was constantly threatening to disappear in new growth. It never did, though, because it was used far too often by Charlie and the family. When they finally broke through the woods, they climbed the slight hill that the house rested upon and stepped onto the back deck. Jim looked in the kitchen window and saw his mom making breakfast. She looked up and smiled at them.

She was the best mom in the world. Karen was a retired nurse, who always knew what to do, and she took such great care of Charlie. Her long, brown hair was held back in a bouncy ponytail. Jim's friends all thought she was really pretty, but she was just "Mom" to Jim. He got irritated when his guy friends talked about how pretty she was.

All he cared about right now, though, was if she was making waffles or not.

Catching a glimpse of his and Charlie's reflections in the sliding glass back door, Jim suppressed a laugh. Though Jim had grown a few inches in the last year, Charlie still towered over him. He flexed his own bronzed, athletic arms in the window, then looked at Charlie's massive arms, and this time he laughed out loud. He was dwarfed by Charlie.

Jim hurried through the back door and stepped into the house. Banjo, the family's Catahoula dog, pounced on him immediately. He was a huge guy, who always looked like he was smiling. Jim loved his gray color with black splotches, but best of all, he liked the white spots he had on his chest, feet and the tip of his tail. That tail was always held high, and many times all Jim could see was that white tail bouncing along as Banjo nosed through the woods. Banjo loved Charlie, too. Charlie bent down to give him some great petting and scratching.

Jim greeted his mom. "Morning! The tent was great." He breathed in the sweet and savory smells of breakfast and looked around the bright kitchen. Jim loved their house. It was always so open and bright.

"Oh good! I'm glad you finally got to use it. Did Charlie sleep inside?" She was whisking some eggs. Jim noticed a bowl of pancake batter ready to go. *Yes!*

"Nah, he likes sleeping outside better. Right, Charlie?" Jim looked up at Charlie, who had stepped through the door and was blocking out much of the light with his massive body. He was wearing a big smile on his hairy face. He looked at Karen and let out a light whoop sound. Pancakes made him happy, but they were also very rich for his stomach, so he had to eat slowly and very little.

"Come on, Charlie. Let's see what Jilly's doing," Jim said.

They walked to the living room but saw no Jilly, so they headed up the stairs. As they turned the corner to ascend the last flight, they could hear Jilly talking in a squeaky voice. "Up and over … that's it!"

Reaching the top of the stairs, Jim saw Jilly making a fluffy, plump, black and white cat do a backflip. "Jilly! Don't do that! That's probably not good for Oreo."

"She likes it. Look! She's even purring," she countered.

Sure enough, Oreo was purring and rubbing her head in Jilly's open palm.

"Weird cat," Jim said. Charlie walked past him and entered the small, pink room.

"Charlie!" Jilly squealed in delight. She jumped up and raised her arms so that Charlie could pick her up. He swooped her up in a large, hairy hug, then set her back down.

Jilly smoothed her waist-length red hair and stared up at Charlie with huge, hazel eyes. Jim knew that she adored Charlie. They both did. She turned her large eyes on Jim, and he saw they were flashing with excitement.

"Dad's coming home early."

"Really? That's awesome."

Jim was thrilled. Their dad, Jack, worked hard. He was in the medical field and owned his own company, so, although he worked hard, he could make time for his family. The Thomas kids loved having their dad home to go exploring through the woods, or go fishing, or have fun in the pool. Pretty much anything as long as it was outdoors.

Now Jim could feel his own eyes gleaming because he had been working on his dirt bike and was hoping for a ride with his dad—the first of the summer. They each had one and would go riding around the woods and neighborhood. It was fun, just Jim and his dad. Of course, Jilly had her own little dirt bike and really could ride with the best of them, but she was never up for long, hard rides through the woods.

Afterward, he wanted to go over his research on Charlie and where he may have come from. He had also been searching for signs of Charlie's family.

"Breakfast!" Karen yelled from the kitchen. Charlie and Jilly followed Jim down the stairs. Jim was starving, but his mind was on his plans for later. He wanted to get Charlie's family back.

Later that afternoon, Jim and Charlie settled down in front of the maps that Jim and Jack had gathered together. Jim had been trying to teach Charlie about maps and what they represented, hoping to figure out where he came from and where his siblings may be. That was his goal: to find Charlie's family.

"So, Charlie, here's what we've got. This here, this is us. See? This is our road, this is our lake." He was pointing and hoping that Charlie was putting things together. Jim began pointing at places on the map that indicated different landmarks and different types of topography, then pointing at pictures that he had found online to show what these were. Charlie seemed to be getting it. He could look at the blue on the map and point at the corresponding picture of a lake on the computer.

Jim started to speak again, but Charlie held up a hand. It was a very human gesture. He stopped and watched Charlie as he studied the map. Charlie's brows knitted together in concentration, and he hunched his large shoulders over the map. Jim stayed quiet for a long time and finally left to talk to his dad.

Finding his dad at the kitchen table, Jim sat down beside him. "Hey, Dad. Charlie's really studying the map. I think he might get it."

"Yeah? That's great. This is the first step." He put down the book he was reading. "How's the research coming?"

Jim had been doing his best to research bigfoot sightings in the state. He had found a lot of information regarding the supposed activity of apparently many bigfoot in the state, but Jim wasn't sure about all of the stories. In fact, he doubted most. There were a handful that he thought could possibly be real.

"Uh … I'm working on it. There are tons of sightings, but who knows how many are real? Only some look real to me. And they're all over the state, but mostly sort of around here. There are a lot in the east between us and Louisiana."

"Interesting. What about wildfires? Since he was probably driven from his home by a fire, I assume it was rather large. At least large enough to make him seek a new home this far away."

This was Jim's idea last year. Charlie had indicated that a fire had separated him from his family. Jim had the idea to look up wildfires in the area and work outward to see where Charlie may have come from. There were only a small amount of fires and really only a couple big enough to force Charlie and his family away.

"There were some big ones a couple of years ago, in the central part of the state. That lines up with some of the sightings."

His dad rubbed his strong chin. Jim watched him think. He was an athletic man, tall and strong, with brown hair and eyes. Jim knew he looked very much like his dad, but his own eyes were gray.

"Maybe we can start there."

"Maybe." Jim was being cautiously hopeful. "But his family would have moved away from the fire, too."

"True."

Jim was worried about how they would actually accomplish this. Their idea was to have Charlie narrow down the direction of his previous home and to travel over the summer to hopefully find familiar areas and eventually his home. From there, they may be able to find his siblings if they had stayed in the area. Of course, they had probably left, just as Charlie had. In that case, they would work their way outward again, but Jim knew that was a real longshot. He had felt silly asking his parents to do this, but they had agreed immediately. Both loved Charlie and both loved to travel. Plus, they had been talking about taking a road trip through the state, so this was perfect.

He sat down and started reading from a bigfoot book he had bought. Despite having the real thing, he wanted to see what others were saying. He wanted to see what the supposed experts were saying. For the most part, they had guessed right. But that wasn't hard to do considering they had very general guesses based on many sightings, and the fact that bigfoot were rarely seen. Anyone could guess that they were secretive, careful around humans, intelligent. What he found interesting was that so many different civilizations had stories about such a creature. To Jim, this meant that there are many of these creatures all around the world.

One thing he disagreed with was the fact that bigfoot are supposed to be only about as intelligent as an ape. Charlie was smarter. Not that Jim knew any apes personally, but from what he knew of them, Charlie was smarter. He understood human interactions and language to a certain extent. Despite his intelligence, Jim doubted he could figure out a map.

He heard Charlie shuffling along the hallway, and then he appeared at the door to Jim's room, carrying the map. Charlie placed it on Jim's lap and sat down heavily on the edge of Jim's bed. It made a U-shape under his bulk. Jim shrugged in his questioning gesture. Charlie just looked back. He didn't get it. Not that Jim had really expected him to. He was a bigfoot after all.

This just meant that they would have to go about it a different way. Jim was looking into certain sighting claims and trying to figure out if any lined up with everything he knew about Charlie. He was concentrating on the few he had found to be most plausible.

One was interesting. It was a farmer in a town called Lakeville, which was situated in the northeast part of Texas. The farmer had seen a tall, hairy creature standing on two feet. He had been working in his vegetable garden and had felt like someone was watching him. He said that he stared at the woods for a while and finally saw a creature that was at least seven feet tall. It had been standing next to a tall oak tree, just watching him. He was shocked but still thought maybe his eyes were seeing something that wasn't there, and then it seemed to melt into the trees behind it. The next day, he found his vegetable garden had been pilfered. He thinks that the creature he saw was stealing his vegetables.

This really struck home for Jim because he had known Charlie to steal vegetables when he was hungry. The other thing was the farmer's description of how the creature melted into the woods. That's exactly how Charlie moved. One second he was there, then the next he was gone, and it was as if he had simply become part of the forest behind him.

This felt like a real encounter.

In doing some more research, Jim had found many more sightings in the surrounding area, and there were supposedly more from Lakeville itself, but people were wary about sharing their own stories. He also found that Lakeville had a lake and lots of creeks. There was plenty of water, woods, and a food supply. Farms and other large tracts of land would give a bigfoot a place to hide without too many people around to discover them.

But the topper? The bulk of the sightings, the most recent sightings, started around the time when Charlie would have been forced out of his home from the fire. This is what set Jim on Lakeville. If they were going to look anywhere, this was the place to start.

Jim looked down at Banjo, who was lying next to his feet, his big eyes watching him. "Banjo, I think I have a plan."

At dinner, Jim told his family about what he had found and where they should go. He sat back, nervously waiting to see what they thought. His eyes flicked to each person sitting at the big, square table. Jilly was humming a little song beside him, his parents were sitting side by side to the left of them, and Charlie was to the right, taking up both seats.

"That's all very logical," Jack said. He sat back in his chair, hands behind his head. "That area would be perfect for a being like Charlie. Plenty of woods, plenty of water, plenty of food, private … or semi-private, at least."

"I haven't been in that part of the state, either," Karen said, always ready for travel.

"Neither have I," Jack agreed. "I guess it's settled: we're going."

Jim smiled. Even though he knew his parents were very easygoing, he still hadn't expected them to jump at this idea right away. He loved their adventurous spirits.

"Charlie, do you like your roast?" Jilly asked. She was picking at hers, making sure any fat was gone.

Charlie looked at her, then chomped down on a huge piece of it. Apparently the roast was something he liked. Of course, he had rubbed off a lot of the spices and gravy. He didn't seem to like too much spice. He was eating veggies but only the raw ones Karen had put out for him. Again, no spices.

It turned out that Charlie ate a lot of food. Being so large, he needed a lot. Karen didn't mind fixing his meals, but it was constant. He also liked to go out and forage for other things, but it was best if he stayed on their property and ate what they got him. It had just been a matter of figuring out what he liked. And really, they were still figuring it out.

"When do you think we'll go?" Jim asked.

Jack thought for a moment. He looked at Karen. "I can get some time off next month. That's only two weeks away. Not much time to get ready."

"Not much time, no, but we can do it. We haven't had a vacation in a while. I think it'll be good for the family and for Charlie."

Charlie looked up at the mention of his name but quickly went back to eating. He was downing a whole watermelon for dessert; the family was splitting another. Jim loved the cool, sweet fruit, too.

"What about Banjo?" Jilly squealed. She looked down at Banjo, who was sitting so nicely beside her, his big eyes begging for a bite of food. Jim watched her put a nice piece of roast on her fork and reach down to Banjo. Amazingly, he gently took the meat off the fork without biting the silverware. He was always so gentle when taking food. "Can we take him?"

"We'll see, but he may need to stay here. We don't know what we'll be doing on this trip, and he may be safer here," Karen said.

"Aww, I'll miss you, Banjo." She almost had tears in her eyes.

They spent the rest of the evening planning their trip. With each passing moment, Jim was getting more and more excited.

It was happening.

CHAPTER TWO
Family Ties

"LET'S GO! WE'RE late!" Jim shouted. He was anxious to get on the road, even though they technically had no specific place to be and in no specific time. He just hated being late when they had set a time.

The two weeks he had waited had been the longest Jim had ever experienced. Since he was done with school, there was nothing he really had to do except wait for their trip. He had packed immediately and even helped Jilly pack, just to make sure she would be ready on time.

And still, they were waiting.

Finally, Karen and Jilly came outside, carrying the last of their personal items. Jim reached out and took Jilly's bag from her to help stow it away in the RV.

"Be careful!" she cried. Her eyes were wide. It was a bit too early in the morning for Jilly, and he could tell she was frazzled and needed sleep, so he was going to tread lightly with her.

"Don't worry, I'll be really careful." He carried it to the back room of the RV, where Karen and Jack would sleep.

The RV was brand new, and this was going to be the first trip in it. Jack had spent weeks learning about it and how to care for it. They had bought it with the plan of taking some road trips, but they didn't know they would be taking Charlie so soon. Jim was looking forward to having their very own traveling hotel.

And it would be perfect for Charlie.

They had taken Charlie inside a few days ago to see how he liked it. Although it was a large space, Charlie still dwarfed it. He looked so big inside, but it was such a nice fit, really. It had to be much more comfortable for him than another vehicle.

Jack had bought a Class C camper that had a fun bed over the cab of the RV. Jim had stowed some of his and Charlie's things up there. It had a couch that folded out into a bed that Jim had claimed because he wanted to sleep next to Charlie, who was going to sleep on a pallet of blankets on the floor. No bed would comfortably hold his bulk and length. Jilly was excited to sleep in her little bed in the folded up dinette area. They had a kitchen, a bathroom and shower, a back bedroom, and the living room area had a slide-out that made the whole space a lot bigger.

The RV packing had taken days. It seemed like they were taking a lot, but Karen said it really wasn't that much. Jim didn't know—he was a light packer. They were taking food for the first few days, but then they would have to stop by a store and get some more. That wouldn't be too bad.

Everyone got seated. Jack was driving, Karen sat next to him, Jim had taken the pilot chair behind her, and Jilly was on the couch. They had Charlie situated on the floor, on a pile of blankets, because he was too big to sit on the couch and not be seen. Jack wanted the blinds open for their first trip so that he could have Jim help him see in case he had trouble starting out. Charlie didn't seem to mind. He had been in the Jeep before and this was much more comfortable for him.

"Ready?" Jack asked.

Everyone yelled out a yes, and they were off.

As they pulled out of the long driveway, Jim got his usual twinge of guilt and sadness at leaving Banjo behind, but he was staying with their aunt and uncle just outside of Houston. They had a small dog that Banjo loved playing with, so he was having more fun than being at the vet. They had told Aunt Kathy they would be gone a couple of weeks, so Jim hoped it wasn't too long for his best buddy Banjo. Jilly had hugged him so tightly that Jim had had to pull her little arms free, but Banjo hadn't seemed to mind.

Jack twisted and turned through their neighborhood, then they were truly off. The RV was louder than a car yet so smooth and comfortable. When they went over bumps, things in the kitchen clanged, but not terribly so, and Jim got used to it quickly.

"This is like driving our house around!" Jilly yelled. She was clapping her hands and looking all around, obviously in a better mood than earlier.

Jim grinned at her. He felt the same way. It was such a fun way to travel. He couldn't wait to really use every feature of this thing.

The first hour of the trip, Jim was afraid to move around. He didn't want to get into trouble or cause any problems for Jack, but he was too excited not to finally move to the dinette after a while. It took a little doing since Charlie was on the floor. Charlie pulled his knees in and moved around to make space for Jim as he passed. Jim pulled out his computer and put it on the table to play games. It was so comfortable!

A loud sound made Jim look to the left. A large truck in the left lane was passing them, and the driver looked over into their RV.

"Charlie, duck!"

But he didn't need to worry, because Charlie was lying down. The man may have seen inside but would have thought Charlie was a stack of blankets.

They took their first stop after a couple of hours and got gas. Jim had to close the blinds so that Charlie would be nicely hidden inside. Everyone stretched their legs, but Charlie had to do the best he could from inside.

Jim took a turn up front with his dad, while Karen played Candyland with Jilly on the couch, in the back.

"Do you think we'll be able to find anything?" Jim asked. He kept asking and knew it probably bothered his parents, but he was worried. He didn't want to be taking them all on a wild goose chase.

"Not sure, but we'll try." Jack looked over at Jim. "Listen, don't worry. We're trying to help Charlie, but we're all having a vacation no matter what. It'll be fun anyway. And it's not just your decision, it's all of ours."

"Okay," was all Jim said. He did feel better and was glad his dad had said that.

They rode along, watching the countryside change. It kept getting more rural. Jim liked looking at the farm houses and all the big swatches of land. At one point, they came to a huge field of yellow wildflowers.

"Look!" he yelled out.

He could hear Karen and Jilly let out some oohs and ahhs.

"These are amazing! They certainly give those famous bluebonnets a run for their money," Karen said. "There's a place further west that so many people go to just to take pictures of the bluebonnets, when these are just as good."

It looked like a painting. Jim tried to snap a quick picture, but they were past it before he could get a good one.

Jilly didn't even sleep. She usually slept the whole ride to anywhere, but this time she was awake. They were taking the long route to their grandmother's house in Palestine, Texas. They hadn't seen her in a while and needed to visit.

Jim hadn't liked the idea of stopping with Charlie, but he wanted to see his grandma, too. He hadn't said anything and was just going to make sure Charlie was as comfortable as possible in the RV, and he promised Charlie he would visit him as often as possible.

"We're close!" Jack announced.

Looking around, things still weren't familiar to Jim, but they usually went a shorter way anyway. Finally, after a while, things started to look more familiar. They were close.

"Here's her street," Jack said as he turned the corner.

They drove along the small street. Little, old houses lined either side, all with unique looks that can only come with time. Grandma's house was on the right, yellow and fading white paint, large porch out front, smaller one to the side by the kitchen. Jim knew there was another porch out back. The house was on pier and beam, which gave it a different look than the houses Jim was used to. He thought it gave it an old-time look. The small yard out front had a stone bench, where Jim and Jilly had posed for pictures the Thanksgiving before last.

Jack pulled into the driveway to the right of the house, and they sat for a moment.

"Okay, so Charlie probably needs a break, but we need to wait until dark," Karen said.

Jim thought he looked a bit uncomfortable, but he realized Charlie hadn't used the bathroom in a while. Charlie was shy in that regard, but they had tried to teach him to use the toilet. He was getting more used to it and would definitely use it if required. And it was required now, because he couldn't go outside. Not now.

"Here, Charlie," Karen said. She was gathering some food for him. In the refrigerator, she had some pre-made sandwiches, some fruit and veggies, and some leftover chicken from the night before. She showed him snacks in the cabinets, then got him some water, and they were off.

Jack led the way, always excited to see his mom. They bounded up the steps, and he opened the kitchen door. A delicious smell wafted to meet them, and Jim's mouth immediately began to water.

"Mom? We're here," Jack called.

Jim heard a soft reply from the front room of the house. They moved into the kitchen and went into the living room to the left, just as Grandma strode into the room.

She was a sturdy woman, who looked like she could handle herself, even at this age. Her hair was white, with some darker gray, and styled like Jim knew other women her age usually wore it— short and somewhat curled. She had large glasses that made her eyes look bigger than they were, but they showed when her eyes sparkled. And when they did, Jim loved it. She had an adventurous side and a sharp mind.

"There you are! I thought I heard someone out there, but I was working on a pattern."

Sewing was something she loved to do, and she would sometimes send them things that she had made for them, like pillows, quilts, once even a pillow-quilt. It was a small throw that folded into a pillow, and she called it a "piller quilt." Jim always laughed inside when he heard that.

She hugged Jack tightly, then moved to give each of the others their own strong hugs.

"Let's go to the kitchen. I've got a brisket I need to check on." She was all business.

Brisket! Jim loved her brisket. And her macaroni. Only one other thing would make the meal perfect. As he walked back into the kitchen, he spotted it on the back counter—her fudge cake. This was going to be the best dinner ever. Jim suddenly remembered Charlie and felt bad that he couldn't be in here with them. He would try to sneak some of the food out later.

The afternoon was spent looking at the house, old pictures, and other relics in the garage. Jim loved all the old stuff. Her house was like a museum of the Thomas family. They gathered in the sewing room, and Jim was now looking at pictures. Jilly was on the floor, looking at sewing stuff.

"Jilly, come here. I made you a shirt," Grandma said from the door.

"Yay!"

Jilly jumped up and ran after their grandmother to get her new prize.

Jim turned back to his pictures. He finished with the box he was working on and started looking along the back wall. There were boxes all over, but they mostly contained odds and ends. No pictures. He moved to the far corner and found a small wooden box beneath a stack of cardboard boxes. He stepped around boxes and other items to get to his new target and then removed the cardboard boxes and opened the wooden one. It had a couple of stacks of old letters, each wrapped in twine.

Carefully taking the first one out of its yellowing envelope, he started reading. He quickly found that it was from Grandma's first husband, who had died in World War II. He felt kind of like he was invading their privacy, but he kept reading. The letters were sweet. Mostly he was telling her about things happening there—training, people, food. It was such an insight into what he went through.

Jim noticed the letters were all crinkled and worn. The second stack was letters from his grandmother to her husband. They must have been returned to her after he died. These were even more fun to read because they really showed a side to his grandmother he had never seen. She had always just been a grandmother to him, but these letters showed a young woman who was in love, missing her husband, and talking about friends, things she did that day, work. She had worked odd jobs here and there.

He was flipping through and found one particularly thick envelope. He opened that one and began reading. It was a full description of daily activities, and she wrote about visiting with her parents. There was also a yellowed newspaper clipping from over fifty years ago. He stopped reading the letter and looked at that.

What he saw made him feel a tingle all over.

The headline read "Large Man-like Creature Terrorizes Women." Jim couldn't read fast enough. Apparently, two young women were driving home from a church event, when they stopped to check a tire that had been leaking air. They heard something in the woods behind them and turned to look but saw nothing at first. The sounds kept coming. They were something like a howl and some yips. The women thought they were being stalked by coyotes or wolves, which was odd but wouldn't be entirely unheard of. They turned back to the car to finish their inspection as quickly as possible. When they got up to leave, they took one more look at the woods.

That's when they saw it.

It was at least seven feet tall, covered in medium-length brown hair. Its arms were huge and spread wide. It stood before them, making gestures and moaning sounds. The women were too terrified to run, but they finally managed to slip back into their car. They say the creature moved toward them, so they sped away, hoping that it wouldn't follow.

Jim was stunned. Why did his grandmother have this? He picked up the letter and continued reading. He skimmed and finally found the part that referenced the clipping.

I've enclosed an article that tells a story that happened to me! You'll be shocked. Susan and I were driving home from church last week and came across some sort of creature that I can only describe as a hairy man. It wasn't human, exactly, but it was something close. I'm not sure what it was. It scared us nearly to death. Remember when we were talking about strange things? This couldn't have been stranger! I'll tell you all about it when you come home, but read the article.

Jim was beyond shocked. His own grandmother had encountered a bigfoot. He stood up and took a few steps to the door, then turned back around and put the letter and clipping back, then picked them up again. He didn't know what to do.

"Jim?" Jack poked his head in the room. "Dinner's ready."

He caught the look on Jim's face. "What is it?"

"You have to see this. Start with the clipping."

Jim pushed the papers into Jack's hands. He realized that he felt a smile plastered to his face.

Jack's eyes flitted over the page. Jim watched them get wider as he read. Finally, he switched to the letter, and Jim pointed out the spot that talked about the incident. Jack started laughing.

"This is incredible."

They stared at each other for a moment, unsure of what to do, each thinking.

"Let's go," Jack said. He turned and led the way to the kitchen. Jim could feel their tingling excitement surrounding them like a cloud of electricity.

When they entered the warm kitchen, Karen and Grandma were moving around the room, getting everything set for dinner. Jilly was sitting in one of the chairs, legs swinging, ready to eat.

"Mom," Jack said. He held up the letters.

She turned around and saw what he was holding.

"You found our letters. You can read them. They might be interesting. We talked about what was happening during those times, how hard it was. You'll learn a lot about him."

"And you," Jim said.

She looked at him. "And me."

"Grandma, we found a newspaper article and a letter. It's about something you saw years ago."

"You're talking about the hairy man I saw."

Karen and Jilly both stopped moving and turned to gape at her.

Jim was surprised. His grandmother was still sharp; nothing escaped her.

"Yes."

She cocked a hip against the counter. "You read the paper?"

"Yes."

"The letter?"

"Yeah."

"Then you know what happened." She shifted back to her work, moving dishes from the counter to the table. "Sit down, eat some brisket. I've got a chocolate cake for dessert." She grinned up at him, her glasses magnifying the sparkle in her eyes.

"But, Grandma. I want to hear it from you."

"Why are you so interested in this?" She was serving out brisket to everyone's plates. Jim noticed she took none for herself.

"I like this sort of thing. It's interesting."

"I'll tell you the story if you help me move some of my plants to the back deck."

"Deal!"

Jim sat down next to Jilly and started scooping massive amounts of her delicious macaroni and cheese onto his plate.

"It happened like the article said, but they sort of exaggerated a bit."

"How so?" Karen asked.

"Well, we were scared, sure. But we were talking about it later, after we got home, and we thought that maybe the thing needed help or something. It was limping a bit and looked confused. I thought it had been hit by a car."

"Really? So it wasn't 'terrorizing' you?" Jim asked.

"I don't think so. It was moaning, too. Sounded awful." She took a bite of macaroni but had nothing else on her plate.

"Poor bigfoot," Jilly said. She was looking around the table, her eyes sad. "Grandma, why do you not eat the other stuff? You cooked it, you should eat it."

Grandma looked at her with a smile. "I like my macaroni."

Nobody had asked her what she thought it was yet. And she hadn't said. She had called it a hairy man.

Jim cleared his throat. "Uh, Grandma."

"Yeah?"

"What do you think it was?"

She set her fork down and continued chewing, her eyes thoughtful.

"Well, I don't know."

Everyone was staring at her, waiting for more.

"It looked like a man, but it didn't. It was huge, bigger than any man I've ever met. We even had a basketball player here from the NBA once, ate at that Mexican place, but this was bigger than him. Wider. I guess I would say it was what Jilly said. A bigfoot."

Silence settled on the table for a moment. Jim's eyes flicked to his parents. Jack was looking at his mom, thoughtful.

He asked, "Do you believe in them? Bigfoot?"

"Well I saw one, so I have to. They exist."

Can't argue with that, Jim thought.

Jim heard a little giggle and turned to see Karen laughing. Sometimes she got into laughing fits, which were always contagious to Jim. She was able to see funny things and they tickled her, which always tickled Jim. All of a sudden, they were all laughing.

Except Grandma.

"What's so funny?" She looked slightly hurt.

"No, no, Mom. We're not laughing at you. We, uh." Jack stopped.

"We have something to … show you?" Jim turned questioningly to his parents.

"Yeah, something to show you," Jack said.

Karen nodded.

"What is it?" Her brows were knitted in confusion.

"It's in the RV."

"Is it something good?"

"Yes. Exceptional," Jim answered. Karen's brows raised in appreciation of his word selection.

"Okay. After dinner. Eat up!"

Jim was annoyed at first but quickly forgot about it enough to thoroughly enjoy his dinner. They had brisket, macaroni and cheese, some delicious bread with butter, and green beans. For dessert, Grandma sliced up her famous fudge cake. It was Jim's favorite. The cake was so rich, and the fudge icing was insanely good. He sat back, feeling full and content.

"So what's this you wanted to show me?" she asked. Jim looked up and saw a glint in her eye.

"Let's go," Jack said.

They made their way outside, and Jim rushed forward to see Charlie first. He went inside and found Charlie sitting on his pile of blankets, eating again. He had a loaf of bread and a jar of peanut butter; his finger was serving as a knife. *Well, that will have to be Charlie's peanut butter now.*

"Charlie! Hey. How are you? Listen, my grandma's coming to meet you. You have to be quiet and nice." He grabbed Charlie's hand and started pulling him to the back of the RV. "Come on. Come back here." It took Charlie a minute to get up and move to the back, and Jim tried to squeeze by him to get in front of him.

A knock sounded on the door and Jim told them to come in. Jilly bounded up the steps and looked at Charlie with dazzling eyes. She was practically shaking with excitement.

Charlie looked down at Jim, his eyes wide with fear. He could hear Grandma talking and coming closer.

"It's okay, Charlie. It's okay," Jim assured him.

Charlie's frightened eyes relaxed a little. He cocked his head to the side in a curious manner.

"Grandma," Jilly called out the door, "Don't be afraid. He won't hurt you. He wouldn't hurt anyone. He loves us and we love him!" She started jumping back and forth between her two feet.

"What are you talking about? Who?" Jim could hear his grandma grab the rail and start up the two steps. Jack was holding her other arm, helping her up.

She stepped up, and Jim moved forward and grabbed her arm from Jack. She steadied herself and began looking around, looking anywhere but the back, where Charlie was.

Charlie looked unsure of himself. He was standing in the doorway between the kitchen area and the back bedroom. He was so large that he was partially inside the open bathroom door. His eyes were darting around to all the family members for reassurance.

Jack and Karen entered quickly, and Jim could see Jack was breathing hard and his eyes were wide. He looked like a little kid.

"Mom, this is Charlie. He's nice."

Jack nodded in Charlie's direction, and Grandma looked in the direction he had indicated. Jim saw her eyes go wide, her mouth went slack. She let out a small "ohh" sound. Jack put an arm around her.

"My word. Oh my ..."

Jim stepped up to Charlie and grabbed his hand. He looked at his grandma.

"Charlie's my best friend. We met him last summer and have been looking after him ever since. We want to help him find his family."

"Dear me ... he's not human, is he?"

"No, he's not like us," Jack answered.

"Can he understand anything I say?"

"He's actually very good at understanding many words, tones. He's extremely smart."

"Come here, son," she said to Charlie, surprising everyone.

Charlie recognized the authoritative tone, but he was shy. Jim motioned him over, and he only hesitated a moment before stepping forward, in a hunch. He paused in front of Jim's grandmother, then began shifting shyly from foot to foot in front of her, his eyes on his feet.

"Well hello there. I'm Margie."

She stared up at him, a slight grin on her face. Charlie looked down at her and his face relaxed, and Jim could see interest and affection replace the worry.

"I can't believe it. Yes!"

Her outburst surprised everyone and made them all laugh.

"I've known all these years that they were real, and now here it is. Proof. People thought I was crazy."

"You're not crazy. At least not about this," Jack said, grinning slyly.

Grandma slapped his arm playfully.

"This is amazing."

She reached up and touched his arm, then his face, grabbed his hands. She was inspecting him, and Charlie didn't seem to mind a bit. After a moment, he reached out and gingerly touched her face. He traced a wrinkle and smoothed out her cheek. Jim realized Charlie hadn't seen anyone as old as she was.

Grandma laughed. Again, it made everyone else laugh. Jim grinned at his parents. He couldn't believe how well she had taken it.

"Well come on inside."

"You want him to come in the house?" Jack asked.

"Of course. I'm not having him sleep out here alone."

She started for the steps, and Jack rushed forward to help her down. They made sure nobody was out and about, turned off the porch lights for a few minutes, and rushed Charlie into the house.

He entered the home and looked all around. The house wasn't as roomy as theirs, so Charlie looked a bit scared of knocking things over or bumping into things. He was stiffly moving about, twisting his head this way and that, trying to keep track of where his massive body was. Jim grabbed his arm and helped guide him around a small, fragile looking table next to her china cabinet.

They maneuvered into the living room and all found seats. Charlie sat on the couch with Jim, Grandma sat in her plush lounge chair, Jack in another smaller chair, and Jilly and Karen sat on the piano bench.

"Does he want some food?" Grandma asked.

"Not sure," Karen answered. Turning to Charlie, she asked, "Want some food?"

His eyes widened. He nodded.

"All right." Karen disappeared into the kitchen to fix him a plate.

"While she does that, tell me how you met him, Jim."

Jim took a breath and began. Before he knew it, the conversation had taken them deep into the evening hours. They had spoken at length about Charlie, bigfoot, and different beliefs. The conversation had turned to other stories Grandma had that nobody had ever heard before. It was a fun evening.

Hearing a great snore, Jim looked at Charlie and found him asleep, with his head lolling to the side, his mouth slightly parted.

"He's pretty tired. First day of traveling, meeting you. He was really excited and nervous when he realized we were gearing up for a trip."

"He's amazing," Grandma said. Her eyes were fixed on Charlie, and she looked serene. For years she had thought she

might be crazy or that people would think she was crazy. This had
to be a nice bit of vindication for her.

"We should all get some sleep," Karen said. Jilly was already
dozing in her lap.

"Can y'all stay one more day?" Grandma asked. Her eyes
hadn't left Charlie.

A look passed between Jack and Karen, something
imperceptible was communicated between them, then Jack nodded
to Grandma.

"Of course. We're in no rush."

Charlie obviously enjoyed their unexpected extended stay.
Grandma treated him like one of the family, getting him snacks and
talking to him. His face never changed from happiness and relaxa-
tion. Grandma's house was small but comfortable, and Charlie
seemed to enjoy it.

Jim noticed how Grandma stayed close to Charlie throughout
the day, constantly talking to him, grabbing his arm, and smiling. If
Charlie had been a person, Jim might have been jealous. But as it
was, he understood her fascination and attention. It wasn't every
day that a bigfoot came into your house, or your lifelong belief that
they existed was finally confirmed.

Grandma made them a hearty breakfast of eggs, bacon, hash
browns, and toast with homemade grape jelly. They spent the
morning looking at old pictures, visiting, and relaxing. Dinner was
brisket again because they had a lot left over, but everyone was
thrilled.

By the time they got ready for bed, everyone was full and sat-
isfied. Jim didn't want to leave, but they had to.

"We'll probably be gone before you get up, Mom," Jack said.

"I figured as much. I'll miss you," she looked around at each
of them, "All of you." Her eyes stopped on Charlie. "Thanks for

bringing him to me. It did my heart good to know that they're really there and good. He's special."

"He is," Karen agreed.

Jim felt good. He felt hopeful, too. This trip was starting out great.

CHAPTER THREE
Road to Discovery

A KNOCKING NOISE woke Jim up the next morning. It was barely light out. He could see blue peeking through the window shades. His eyes didn't want to stay open, but the noise came again, so he got up and stumbled out of the room he was sharing with Jilly and his parents.

Charlie was sitting up on the couch in the living room and greeted Jim with a wave. The noise came again, and this time he could tell it was from the kitchen.

Jim, still stumbling, made his way into the kitchen and rubbed his eyes. His grandmother was packing up a cardboard box with containers of food. She looked up at the sound of his feet scuffing the linoleum.

"Hey. You should still be sleeping."

"What are you doing? I thought you were going to sleep."

"I couldn't sleep. Been too excited. I wanted to pack y'all some food. Charlie's been keeping me company. I just sat him down with a Popsicle a few minutes ago."

Jim turned and saw Charlie holding a small wooden Popsicle stick. He had been too sleepy to notice it before. Charlie looked like he didn't know what to do with it, so he was just holding it. Jim walked over and put out his hand. Charlie passed it over, looking grateful.

"He likes those things, huh?" she said, giggling. Jim still wasn't used to her giggling like that. It was fun.

"Everyone will be up in a few minutes. We're leaving early. Need help?"

"I'm just about finished. I didn't want this food to waste, so you can put it in your refrigerator in that fancy camper."

Jim smiled. "Any of that chocolate cake?"

"Of course!"

"What's all the racket?"

Jim turned to see Jack and Karen walking through the door, both squinting their sleepy eyes.

"Morning, sleepyheads." Grandma winked at Jim.

"Grandma's putting together some food for us. She even packed the rest of the cake," Jim informed them.

"Thanks, Margie." Karen smiled gratefully.

They ate a small breakfast of cereal and fruit. Jilly slept in, but that wasn't unusual. She just wasn't a morning person. Still, Jim felt bad letting her miss Charlie's last bit of time with Grandma and tried to wake her, but she was dead weight when he tried to lift her by her arms.

Karen and Jack worked on packing things back up in the RV, so Jim sat with his grandmother at the kitchen table. Charlie was standing against the counter in such a human-like stance that it made Jim do a double take. He looked so casual, leaning back with his right foot crossed over his left. Jim let out a small laugh.

"He's your best friend, huh?" Grandma's voice cut into Jim's thoughts.

"Yeah, he really is."

"You're worried he'll leave you if he finds his family?"

"A little." Jim hadn't admitted that to anyone.

She looked up at Charlie for a moment.

"He won't. He's as attached to you as you are to him."

That made Jim feel lighter, better.

"Why didn't anyone wake me?" came Jilly's voice from the doorway, thick with sleep.

"I tried!"

Jim always told her how he tried, but she never believed him, because she never remembered.

She grumbled something at him and went to hug Grandma and Charlie.

The rest of the time there went by in a flash. They hurried around, getting everything packed up and trying to get Charlie out of the house before it was too light out.

Jim and Karen sat on the porch for a few minutes, watching things. Not too many people were out and about yet, so they had time. Going back inside the kitchen, they found Grandma sitting next to Charlie, having a quiet word with him.

Not wanting to intrude, they quietly moved through to the living room and waited. Jim wanted so badly to hear what she was saying to him, but he knew better than to pry. Her eyes were kind and her voice soft. Charlie probably had little idea of what she was saying, but he looked very intent and like he was enjoying the kind attention.

Finally, the quiet murmur stopped, she patted his arm, and they went back into the kitchen. Both Grandma and Charlie stood, and Jack and Jilly came clattering through the kitchen door, having loaded the last of the bags.

"Everyone ready?" Jack asked.

Karen looked around. "Yep, looks like it. Oh, Margie, thanks so much for everything." She hugged her tightly.

Everyone stepped forward to thank Grandma and hug her before they left. Jim waited until last. He wasn't much for hugging, normally, but he did want to hug her. Everyone was headed to the door, Jack in the lead, ready to help sneak Charlie out of the house.

He had maneuvered the RV as close to the house as he could get and had the door ready.

"Jim, I love ya."

"Love you, too, Grandma." He felt uncomfortable, but he wanted her to know how much he had appreciated her kindness to Charlie and just being his grandmother.

She must have seen his dilemma, because she grabbed his hand and said, "I know. Thanks for sharing him with me. I've had fun with all of y'all."

Then they were all piled in and waving goodbye to Grandma, who was watching them leave from the porch.

Jim felt his usual moment of sadness as he saw her turn and walk back into the house alone. She was such a tough lady, but he hoped she wasn't lonely. He vowed to have his family visit her more often, although he knew she had an active role in the church, which took a lot of her time. She wasn't lonely.

The ride began the usual way—Jilly asleep in the chair behind the passenger seat, mouth hanging open, Karen and Jack up front, Jim trying to stay awake and help navigate. Charlie was lying back on his pallet, napping. Who knows what time Grandma got up, but Charlie had been up with her. He had to be tired.

Too soon they were pulling into a wildlife park near his grandmother's home and trying to get Jilly to wake up. They had planned to visit this place at the last minute when Jim's grandmother mentioned that something strange had been seen there a couple of years ago. This had been news to Jim, but he imagined that a lot of sightings didn't get reported to places that posted them on the Internet.

As they drove along, the whole family pressed their faces to the windows to see the thick, inviting foliage. It was, as Karen would say, scenic, but seeing places like this mostly made Jim want to explore the woods. He was sure there was plenty of cool stuff hiding out there, waiting to be discovered.

"Jack, get the park pass out," Karen reminded him, but he was already digging out his wallet from the center console. They had an annual pass, so they would be able to get through the entrance quickly.

They pulled to the window, and a woman dressed in her khaki park uniform greeted them cheerily.

"Hello. Checking in or just staying the day?"

Waiting to get through, Jim saw a car in the lane next to theirs. A family was sitting inside while the dad was adjusting some things on the roof and looking like he was having a hard time. He was dressed in new-looking khaki clothes and some hiking boots. Obviously, he had done some shopping for their little excursion. The two small kids in the back were being rowdy, fighting over a toy, while the mom yelled at them from the front. On the other side of them was the biggest fifth wheel RV Jim had ever seen. It had at least five slide-outs and a place in the back that would hold some sort of recreational vehicle, like an ATV or golf cart. He couldn't imagine what they had in there, but he wanted to see inside.

"Look at that! That thing's huge!"

Everyone pressed their faces to the windows for a look at the monster RV. Charlie popped up to take a quick peek before Jim could tell him to stay down. The little boy in the car next to them had stopped fighting with his little sister and was looking grumpily out the window, obviously having lost the fight. As soon as Charlie popped up in the window, the kid's eyes shot over to him, and Jim watched amazement come over him. His eyes and mouth popped open like a kid seeing Santa, and Jim could just feel his excitement. He started pointing, and turned to yell something to his family, but Jim had already nudged Charlie back down.

"Uh-oh. Charlie's been made," Karen said, with a hint of amusement in her voice.

When he turned back, a different type of surprise spread over his face. As Jim watched, the boy's features drooped and his brows scrunched together in confusion and disappointment. His eyes searched each window of their RV and finally met Jim's eyes. All Jim did was raise his own eyebrows, then Jack pulled them forward, and they were gone. Karen started laughing and the rest of the family joined in. Poor kid.

They drove to the conservation center and parked to the far side of the lot. Jack turned on the generator and got the air conditioner going.

"Who wants to stay with Charlie?"

"I will," Karen offered. "I need to rearrange some things that I heard clunking around back there."

She got up and started for the back room to adjust some mementos Grandma had sent with them.

Jack, Jim, and Jilly hopped out and went into the small, neutral-colored building. It was squat and simple, basically the same design as the buildings in the state park near their home. A tinkling sounded above them as they entered, and the portly gentleman behind the counter scurried to get his book put away and look welcoming.

"Hello! Can I help you with anything in particular?"

Jim looked at Jack. They had wanted to find out about the sighting, but they didn't want to draw too much attention to themselves.

Jack answered, "No, thanks. We're just looking around. Great park you have here."

"Thanks. We love it." The man puffed up with the compliment.

Jilly ran forward to check out the souvenirs they had, and Jim went to the books they had on the shelf. Jack started looking at a map.

There was another man dressed in what Jim thought was bird watching gear. He had the olive Columbia shirt and pants, a khaki vest with a lot of pockets, a pair of binoculars, and a camera. The man glanced up at them as they entered but quickly went back to examining a bird book.

Finally, Jack causally asked, "What's the deal with the bigfoot sighting y'all had?"

The park employee's eyebrows knitted together, and he pursed his lips. "I'm not sure I know what you're talking about. Did someone see something strange out here?"

He had no idea. Jim glanced at the bird watcher, who had stopped his flipping through the book and was watching the proceedings.

"Oh, I heard from my mom that some campers had seen something strange out here. She joked with us about it when she heard we were coming here."

The man perked up. "Oh, that's funny. Funny lady."

He thought it was just a joke on her part. They weren't getting anything out of him.

"Well, thanks. We're off for a hike." Jack gestured with his chin, "Come on, guys."

They left the building and were walking back to the RV when the tinkling sound came again. Jim looked back to see the bird watcher coming toward them. He waved at Jim.

"Hey! Excuse me?"

He hurried up to the family, in a sort of shuffling manner. Apparently he wasn't in the best of shape.

"How can we help you?" Jack asked.

The man stopped, puffing like he had just run a 5k. "Well, I heard you asking about, ah, you know." He wiped his face with a handkerchief. "I'm kinda into that stuff myself. You know, strange things." He looked at them expectantly. Jim guessed he wanted confirmation before he continued.

Jack caught it, too. "Oh yeah. My son and I find that kind of stuff interesting. My mom was telling us about some stories. But what have you heard?"

The man looked around, wide-eyed, jumpy, clearly not used to talking about such things to strangers.

"Oh, well, I, uh, I listen up for things, and I heard the same thing your mother heard, except that it wasn't here. At least, if it's the same sighting, that is. I did hear that some campers had seen something near Bisby."

"Oh yeah? Where's Bisby? I've never heard of it," Jack said.

"It's a very small town. I'll show you on the map."

He pulled out a map from one of his vest pockets and began pointing out directions. Bisby was maybe a couple of hours east from where they were.

"Well, thanks for the info. We'll see if we can swing by there." Jack put out his hand.

The man shook it. "If you do and you hear anything, would you mind sending me an email? Here's my card."

"Sure thing," Jack said. He turned around to leave, and Jim followed.

"What does the card say?"

"Looks like he's the CEO of a computer company. You never know who will be a bigfoot fan. Seems like from all walks of life."

Jilly hurried up to her dad and grabbed his hand. She skipped alongside him, his arm being yanked around by her jerking movements.

"Daddy, where are we going next?"

Jack looked at Jim. "Bisby?"

"Bisby."

CHAPTER FOUR
Bisby

THEY PULLED INTO a gas station on the outskirts of
Bisby for gas and snacks, and Jim could see many trucks in the lot.
That's much of what you saw in these rural areas—trucks. There
was also a black van with green lettering. As he got out, Jim was
looking at the van because he liked the colors together and wanted
to see what the van was.

He walked around the front of the RV, toward the door of the
gas station, and saw that the van had a picture of what looked like
an angry ape on it. The face was large, hairy, and snarling. Sharp,
pointed teeth were visible, and the eyes were dark and menacing.
Its arms were raised in attack, with long, dangerous-looking claws.
Jim suddenly realized that it was a bigfoot. The side of the van said
Bigfoot Crew. Jim had heard of them. They were a team that hunted
for signs of bigfoot and were hoping for a TV show. Right now
they had a website and blog, with lots of videos documenting their
research, and Jim thought they might be on a small local TV
station.

"Dad, look." He pointed at the van.

Jack looked up and narrowed his eyes. "Oh great. I see we have experts here. Maybe they can teach us a thing or two, eh?" He bounced his eyebrows and grinned. "Guess that means we're on the right track."

"Let's see why they're here," Jim suggested.

"Good idea."

First, Jim helped his dad fill up the RV again. As they stood, Jim looked around. This was one of those little towns where everyone knows everyone and the big restaurant is a Sonic. Jim kind of liked these sorts of places. They felt like they had history, and the people in them had maintained a more simple way of life.

They walked into the old store, and Jim quickly spotted the crew. They looked so out of place in the run-down store. It looked like it had been there about a hundred years, and the people inside all looked alike. And they were staring. At the crew and Jim and Jack.

The crew appeared oblivious to the stares and were stuffing their arms full of snacks and drinks. Jim recognized the "star" of the show, Shawna Pepper. She was fairly tall, thin, and pretty, in a kind of nerdy way. Her skin was smooth and fair, her hair was curly, brown, and just past her shoulders. Despite her attractiveness, Jim found her unappealing. She had a smug attitude and seemed to think a lot of herself.

Jim and his dad walked forward and began grabbing snacks and drinks as well. Jim was walking down the aisle that Shawna was on and kept giving her sideways glances. He was wondering what she had actually ever seen. Had she seen a bigfoot before?

Shawna looked up and caught Jim looking at her. She gave him a slight smile and jerked her head up in a little nod. "Hey, dude."

Jim thought it was a rather lame greeting, but he said, "Hi." He couldn't help himself, so he asked, "Ever really seen a bigfoot?"

"Ah, a fan! And I'm not even on TV yet! Well, real TV. Nice to meet you. This is my crew. The big guy's Pete, our videographer, and the skinny guy's Larry, our producer."

Jim looked behind her and saw Pete grinning at her from behind an arm-full of what looked like those pink Sno Ball cake snacks. He was a big guy with a shaved head and a slack jaw. Larry, on the other hand, was skinny as a rail. He looked like skin hanging on bones, with stooped shoulders and a pointed nose. Everything about him was angular. His eyes were darting and never lighted too long on one place.

"So, have you?" he pushed.

Shawna's smile faltered slightly, and she flipped her hair back over her shoulder. "We're confident that we will soon have our proof." She stared into his eyes, daring him to contradict her.

Jim wasn't bothered. "How can you be confident?"

She sighed and eyed Jim carefully, seeming to take better stock of her adversary. "That's really confidential right now, but I can say that we have good reason to believe that one is in the area." She began walking coolly up to the front of the store.

"Where?"

She stopped and looked back. "I can't tell you that. You'll just have to watch for me on TV and see!" With that, she flashed him a brilliant smile that Jim knew she thought belonged on TV.

Pete slid by Jim, with a conspiratorial grin on his round face. As he pulled even with Jim, he leaned in and whispered, "Heh, hey kid, wanna see a bigfoot? Heard of the Hoke Farm? That's where he is." He winked and trudged off to the counter.

Jim looked after him and met his dad's eyes. Jack had been watching from a distance and now walked up to Jim. "What did he say?"

"He said they're going to Hoke Farm. There's a bigfoot there, supposedly."

Jack cocked his head thoughtfully. "Maybe we should stop by. You know, since we're such big fans." He looked at Jim.

"Hey, yeah. We could try that."

"Let's find out about this farm. It's in Bisby?"

Jim shrugged. He helped his dad grab the items they needed, and they carried everything to the counter just as the TV crew was walking out the door. An older man, who looked weather-worn but happy, was standing behind the counter with his hands in his pockets. All three of them watched the crew go. They heard the tinkle of the little, old bell on the door, and then Jim and Jack set their things on the counter.

"Hello there. You hunting for bigfoot, too?" He had an amused expression on his face as he began ringing up their items. He did it the old fashioned way, with no scanner, just a register.

"Actually, we were just passing through. But my son and I have been curious. We hadn't heard about the sightings here. Are they true?"

"Depends on who you ask. Mr. Hoke, sure, they're true. Says he's seen a big ol' thing walkin' through those woods of his. Mrs. Templeton, though, she's very against this stuff."

"Who's Mrs. Templeton?" Jim asked.

"She's this old gal who lives up near the Hokes. She's very, uh, against outsiders. She doesn't want anyone runnin' their mouths about somethin' mysterious bein' out here and attractin' a lot of outsiders."

"Oh. She definitely won't like those TV people." Jim didn't think she sounded like anything to worry about, but he could see how someone may not want their simple life ruined by a bunch of crazy people coming to hunt near their house.

"Mr. Hoke—is he allowing the TV crew to run around their property?" Jack asked.

"Mr. Hoke don't live there anymore. Still owns the land, but he moved when Betsy died. Couldn't stand to live there anymore, even though it's been in the family for over a hundred years. Since he ain't here, he don't mind makin' some money from those people, long as they don't mess nothin' up." He turned and spit into something. Jim stood up on his toes and was able to see that the man had actually just spit into a spittoon. He couldn't believe it.

"Have you seen anything?" Jim asked.

The man looked at Jim and seemed to be deciding on something. "Much as I don't like sayin' it, I did see somethin' a few months back. In all my years, I never seen nothin' like it before."

Jim was excited. "What was it?"

"Not sure, son. All I can say, it looked like a big, hairy fella."

"Awesome!"

Jack looked at Jim and then smiled at the man. "Thanks for your time."

When they got back into the RV, they looked at each other. "This might be the place!" Jim said.

"What happened?" asked Karen. She was sitting at the kitchenette table and writing notes in her little travel log.

"Did you see that van parked over there?" Jack asked.

"Where?" She was now craning her neck this way and that, looking for the van that was already gone.

"Well, it was over there. It had that TV crew from that show I was telling you about," Jim explained. "They're here looking for a bigfoot!"

Jilly gasped excitedly. "They're here! They're here!" It reminded Jim of a less-creepy version of the girl in the movie *Poltergeist*.

Jim heard a noise from the back room. The small door opened, and Charlie's face appeared in the doorway.

"Hey, Charlie! We might have the place." Jim smiled at him. Charlie smiled back, but it looked like he had no idea why Jim was so excited.

Karen got up and reached over Jim. She came up with Charlie's fruit snacks and handed the bowl over to him to munch on. Looking at Jim, she said, "I made sandwiches. They're on the counter."

Jim hadn't even noticed. "Thanks, Mom."

She smiled at him. "So, is this the place?"

Jim and Jack looked at each other. Jack answered, "I think so."

"Let's find a place to stay and get settled," she suggested.

After consulting his phone, Jack found an RV park nearby. Surprisingly, it was pretty nice. The whole place was nestled in the beautiful woods, just off the main road. It had nice sites for the RV, with smooth, solid pads to park on, and grass and trees everywhere, in a pleasing arrangement. Their site was in the far corner, with nobody else nearby. It looked like they were spacing all the vehicles well apart since it wasn't at full capacity, in order to give everyone some privacy. Jack had requested the far corner since it had two trees around it, and the doors they would be using faced away from most everyone.

They parked and got everything hooked up—water, electricity, bathroom. Meanwhile, Karen started setting up their tent so Charlie could get outside and stretch his legs. It was large enough to entirely enclose the picnic table and the area just outside the RV, like the kind that people often used for outdoor parties. They put it next to the door of the RV, so they could go in and out, hopefully without being seen. Jilly was entertaining Charlie inside with a game of Jacks on the floor of the RV. Jim could hear her trying to teach him the game and squealing with delight when she won.

They were finally done, and Charlie gladly ventured outside and stood up straight. He stretched his arms and arched his back. Breathing in deeply, Charlie seemed happy. Jim watched him for a moment and quietly hoped they were successful here.

Jack went to the RV park office and picked up some maps of the area. He also found out that the TV crew would be staying in the bed and breakfast down the street for a few days. It was the big news across the town, according to the man in the office. Back at the RV, he laid out one of the maps, and they located Hoke Farm, two miles down the main road from them. It was well over a hundred acres of farm land, at the end of Main Street. Since it had been there longer than most other buildings and homes, it was situated closer to the town than the others, and at one point, it had been the main source of work for many families.

"What do you say we take a walk?" Jack asked.

"Let's go," Jim answered.

"We'll stay here and get things set up," Karen said. Jilly was sitting on the picnic table, chatting with Charlie, who was listening politely.

Jim and Jack walked down the path to the entrance of the RV park and turned right on the street. They moved into the main part of Bisby and saw that there wasn't much there. There was a small restaurant, pharmacy, city hall, market, even a tiny movie theater. Downtown Bisby was surrounded by houses, and farther down the highway were a couple of fast food places. They passed through the main part of town and kept moving.

The road was the kind of old asphalt that was cracked and had black patch lines in it. The town was fairly quiet. There wasn't that hum of a bigger city. Jim was enjoying the relative quietness. Some people, he knew, considered the rural life to be louder than the city life. There were insects, frogs, birds, and other things that made plenty of noise. But Jim found it to be more natural and more enjoyable than the city noises of car traffic, people talking, building noises, and whatever else created that electric hum.

"Look, there's a sign," Jack said. He had spotted an old wooden sign with faded yellow lettering that declared that Hoke Farm was just up the road. It advertised livestock and vegetables.

"Looks old. I like it," Jim said.

"Yeah, history is fun."

They kept walking and passed a small shop advertising hair cuts by Sally. It looked to be a small home that doubled as a business. An older woman, who may have been Sally herself, was sitting outside on a small, dilapidated porch. Despite the wear and tear, the house shop was actually fairly tidy and inviting. Sally, if that's who she was, was plump and had a warm smile on her face. She reminded Jim of what Mrs. Santa looks like in all the cartoons and movies, only more country. She raised a hand in a friendly wave.

Jim and his dad waved back. "Probably doesn't see too many strangers around here," Jack said. "She seems thrilled to see new faces."

"Yeah. Must be weird."

They kept going and a wooden fence popped up behind the trees that had been lining the roadway. It was a very old-fashioned split-rail fence that had supports, like something out of a Western movie. Beyond the fence, they saw what was once many acres of pastureland. A little ways down the road, they could see a wooden gate to what had to be the farm. It was one of those large wooden entrances that had a home-made sign hanging from it, telling all those who pass that they had found Hoke Farm.

Jim and Jack walked up to the entrance and looked at the driveway beyond. It was long and winding, disappearing behind another stand of trees and reappearing in the distance at the old Hoke Farmhouse. The house was a two-story Victorian mansion with wrap-around porches on both stories of the home. Hoke Farm was a unique blend of trees and pastureland that had a very secretive feeling to it. The house itself was surrounded by a small, understated, white picket fence. Like everything else around here, it had an old, historic atmosphere.

Jim thought it was spectacular.

"Now that's Texas history right there," Jack said. He was staring appreciatively at the house and the sprawling land. Jim was reveling in the feeling of the place. If there really was a bigfoot here, Jim could see why.

Jim let his eyes roam beyond the house, to the right, where there appeared to be another driveway leading back toward the trees. There, he could see the black van with green writing on it. The TV crew was here.

Jim jabbed his dad and pointed to the van. "They're already hunting."

"Yep. This is probably the perfect place for them to look. Seems like a quiet spot with lots of places to hide. I bet there's plenty of water back there and places for a bigfoot to sleep. After all, they raised cows here and the cows need water and places to go when it's too hot, cold, whatever."

"Yeah," Jim agreed. He wanted to get in there. "How do we look around in there without attracting attention?"

"Not sure yet. Let's go back and regroup."

They walked back to the RV park, taking a slower look around the town, and noticed the restaurant seemed to be getting busy. It looked like the place where everyone gathered at the end of a long day. It was probably where many folks around here got their nightly meal.

As they walked up to their campsite, they noticed that people were sitting outside of their RVs or trailers, enjoying the evening and chatting. Almost everyone waved as Jim and his dad passed by.

"They're friendly," Jim commented.

"Yeah. Let's hope they don't get too friendly. They may not appreciate our … friend." Jack gave him a wink.

When they reached their RV, they opened the privacy tent they had constructed and found Karen making up the picnic table. She had some chips and dip sitting on it, and a plate of fruit and vegetables.

"Appetizers. Want to grill the hotdogs tonight?" she asked.

Jack answered, "Actually, I thought we might want to head over to the restaurant and pick up something from there tonight. See if the crew shows up or someone has some information that may be useful. What do you say?"

"I don't want to leave Charlie."

"Right. So only a couple of us have to go."

Jim and his mom were voted to go. She wanted to see the town anyway. She always liked small towns. Jilly was content staying there with Charlie and her dad. They were going to play some games and watch TV.

After a break, Jim and Karen headed down the driveway, through the RV park, and turned right on the main road. Jim led the way, pointing things out to his mom that he had seen during the walk before. After a few minutes, they saw the restaurant. A neon sign proclaimed it to be Mel's Country Diner. It appeared even busier than when he and his dad had seen it. There were mostly trucks in the parking lot, but all of the cars were covered in a thin sheet of dust—the kind that seems to find every vehicle in rural areas. There were a couple with the words "Wash me" scrawled with a finger on the back.

As they approached Mel's, Jim could hear some country music growing louder. He opened the door for his mom, and they entered. The noise seemed to hit them as they came through the door. The music was at a decent volume, but the customers were talking way above it. They all seemed to know each other and were bustling around, talking to different people, saying hi to anyone they knew. There was a haze of smoke on the left side of the building, where a sign indicated it was the smoking section.

"Help ya, hon?" an older waitress asked Karen. She had permed gray hair that made a bubble around her head. Her makeup was like on TV—blue eyeshadow, pink lips, dark mascara. She had plates in each hand and a couple more somehow stacked precariously on her forearms. Obviously, she was on her way to serve a table their dinner.

"Do you do to-go orders?" Karen asked.

"Sure thing. Over at that counter there." She nodded to a small counter at the right. It was next to the drink machine and had a girl of about sixteen working behind it. She had her elbows on the counter and her chin in her hands, obviously bored with her summer job. Karen led the way to her counter, and the girl straightened while her eyes roamed over the both of them.

"May we see a menu?" Karen asked. The girl gawked for a moment and then turned to find a menu. Apparently they weren't used too often, because it was underneath a pile of magazines. The regulars probably knew the menu by heart.

"Need any help, don't hesitate to ask me. I know this place real well." She gave Jim a wink and began inspecting her nails.

"This is probably a fun summer job," Karen commented to her. "Lots of people to visit with."

The girl looked up from her nails. "Oh sure. I just wish I wasn't still in school. Our school is always, like, the last one out. It's so not fair," she whined.

Karen and Jim turned to the menu. It was thick and covered with plastic, but it had a nice, clean look to it. There was nothing spilled on it. The menu claimed that Mel's was eighty years old and had been run by the same family throughout the years. Jim could believe it. In fact, the menu seemed just as old. The food sounded delicious, though—old-fashioned comfort food.

They ordered Jack a chicken-fried steak dinner, Karen got a turkey sandwich with chips, Jim ordered the meatloaf dinner, and they got Jilly the chicken nuggets. They even ordered Charlie a fruit plate, side veggies, and whatever the "Huge Chicken Salad" was. Jim's mouth was watering. He had to admit, the food he was smelling and seeing was making him starving.

He sat beside his mom next to the to-go counter and surveyed the room. Everyone was just like you would see in any small town. They were happy-looking country people, who seemed to be having a great time with each other in the diner. All except the table in the far right corner. These were the TV crew, and they appeared to be deep in conversation. The three of them were leaning forward, heads together, while Shawna was talking non-stop.

Jim nudged his mom and pointed at their table. She narrowed her eyes as she studied them and then nodded.

"Y'all know them?"

Jim looked up to find the to-go girl staring at him.

"Uh, no. We met at the gas station today. I've seen their website," Jim answered.

"Oh, I thought maybe y'all were with them. I never heard of them before." She looked over at them like they were really famous Hollywood stars, which they certainly were not.

"Nah. They say they're here hunting a bigfoot. Have you ever seen one?"

The girl's head snapped back to Jim. "They're lookin' for it? I haven't seen it, but my boyfriend says he has. I don't think he really did, but he says so. I know a guy who swears he saw somethin', though."

Jim liked hearing about another sighting. This could be good. "What did he see?"

"Well, it was late one night a few months back, and Johnny Clifton—he runs the hardware store—he was up in those woods near the Hoke's place. He saw somethin' big, hairy, and standin' up like a man. He was out huntin' and that thing walked up to his bait, sniffed around, then ran off into the woods! Johnny came back hollerin' about what he saw, and a bunch of guys went off lookin' for it. They never saw it again."

"Wow, sounds exciting," Karen said. She looked at Jim with a knowing half-smile.

"Yeah. Wish I could see something like that." Jim was laughing inside. He looked back at the TV crew's table, with an idea forming in his mind.

He turned to his mom. "I'm gonna go talk to them."

"All right. Hopefully the food will be ready soon."

Jim got up and walked straight to the table. Along the way, he could feel the eyes of nearly everyone in the diner following him. It was such a small town. He realized that the TV crew table wasn't the only group that didn't quite belong. There was a table toward the back of the room that gave him a creepy feeling. There were three men sitting, all facing the TV crew, with their eyes locked on Jim as he passed through the room. Their faces were not open and friendly by any means. Jim shook off the chill from their stare and walked up to the TV crew.

"Hey," he said. The three people at the table jumped at his voice.

"Oh, hey. It's our fan," Shawna said. She sat back, looking pleased to have someone recognize her.

"Sup, dude," Pete said. Jim couldn't think of anyone he knew who said "sup" for real these days.

"Did you see anything today?" He got right to the point.

Shawna narrowed her eyes. She seemed to be appraising him, deciding what she should say.

"No ... but we did hear some interesting things."

"What kind of things?"

She took her time answering again. "We heard typical sounds that might be associated with a sasquatch."

"And what would those be?"

"Geez, kid! You said you watch my video blogs. Don't you know what the typical sounds are?" She was looking exasperated with him. Pete had an amused grin on his face, while Larry had his usual frenetic movements going. His eyes were shooting everywhere, and his knees were obviously jumping, because there was a periodic bump from under the table.

"What did you hear?" Jim wanted to know exactly what they heard—or claimed to have heard—and wasn't going to let Shawna push him around.

Shawna sighed. "Okay. We heard some typical hoots and some whooping-type sounds. They're thought to be mating calls."

Jim was pleased. He was all too familiar with the whoops that she claimed to have heard. He remembered back when he had first heard that distinctive whooping sound a year ago. It was a sound that was hard to describe. It was almost like a human making a strange yelling noise, but it was distinctly ... inhuman. He also wasn't sure that it was a mating call. Jim thought it was more like Charlie had been searching for his family or another of his kind. He was asking if anyone was out there.

"That's amazing. I'm really impressed. You guys are really good at your jobs. I'm sure you'll hit it big really soon."

Shawna's face began to glow. She was eating up the praise.

Jim continued. "I want to do what you guys do someday. Maybe one day I could join your crew." He tried to look humbled to be in front of them and passionate about what he was saying.

It was hard.

Shawna seemed to love it. She grinned and looked at her crew.

Pete was grinning back. "This kid's great. He's like our mascot!" he said.

Shawna looked at him. "A mascot ..." She turned back to Jim. "That's an idea. You want to come along tomorrow, maybe two days? Nobody else out there has the kid audience. We could have you be our, let's see ... Junior Investigator! That would be great. Nobody else has that."

Jim couldn't believe it. This was just what they needed. He was really only hoping to be kept in the loop each evening, but this was more than he had hoped for.

"Could I really? That would be awesome." He didn't have to work to look hopeful, because he really felt it.

"Sure. Have to ask your parents, and they'll have to sign a waiver, but I think this will be great!" Shawna was already digging in her briefcase, rifling through papers. She came up empty. "Well, I'll find one for tomorrow. Look, we're going out to Hoke Farm tomorrow at eight o'clock. You have your parents bring you there by seven to sign the papers and get you all set up, okay?"

"Okay. Thanks!" Jim smiled and shook her hand.

He turned and wove his way through the tables, with eyes on him the whole way again. His mom was waiting with the bags of food.

"Perfect timing. I just checked everything. Smells good. What happened?" she asked.

"I'll tell you outside." Jim grabbed a bag from his mom and led the way out the door.

As they walked down the street, Jim told Karen about his conversation. She was a bit skeptical of the whole idea.

"I don't really want my son walking around with those people in some strange woods. Anything could happen, and it would be up to those guys to help you. Have they ever actually been in the woods? Are they experienced with wildlife?"

"Mom, I'm thirteen. I'll be fine. They don't want anything happening to me either, because that would ruin their chances of getting on TV. I'm sure they'll be extra careful."

"We'll talk to your dad. Maybe he can go along."

The rest of the trip was taken in silence, with the occasional "look at that" exclamation. The cicadas were out in full force, creating a natural theme song for their walk.

When they returned, everyone gathered at the picnic table to eat. Jim told the rest of the family about his encounter with the TV crew and their proposal.

Jack's eyes gleamed.

"That's perfect!" he said. "I couldn't have done it any better myself. That's a great plan. That way we get onto the farm and look around. We'll have to figure out the rest as we go along, depending on what we see or hear."

"That's what I thought," Jim agreed.

"You think he'll be okay with those people? They don't seem to be the most mature from what Jim's said about their show," Karen said.

"Sure. I think he'll be fine. I don't think they can let him go without a parent, so we'll make sure that's what happens."

They enjoyed their perfectly down-home, country dinner while talking and listening to the cicadas surrounding them. The windows of the canopy had been covered, but Jim went over to one and peeked out. He could see lightning bugs dancing all around in the darkness of the woods behind them. They always gave him a peaceful feeling.

Sensing someone behind him, Jim looked over his shoulder at Charlie, who had come to take a look. Jim knew that staying inside all of this time was hard for him, but he also knew that it was necessary. Charlie had been extremely anxious lately and really seemed to be missing his own family. If anyone in Jim's family had gone missing, he would do anything to find them. He had to help Charlie.

The family got ready for bed. Before sleep, they waited until they could hear the campground grow quiet. It was easy to hear little things in a campground. Their neighbors on either side were fairly far away and couldn't really see the back of their tent and RV, but they wanted to be careful anyway. When they felt secure, Jack went outside and took a look around. He popped his head back inside and gave Jim a thumbs up. Turning to Charlie, Jim smiled. He took Charlie's massive hand and led him outside.

Charlie ducked his head and exited the tent. In the slight moonlight, they could see Charlie stand up tall, and Jim heard him take a deep breath of air. It must be nice for him to be able to stretch and get outside.

"Good feeling, huh, Charlie?" Jim asked. Jack winked at Jim, then led the way into the woods behind their RV.

Charlie's footsteps were always surprisingly silent to Jim. He had to weigh hundreds of pounds, but he could move through as silently as a small animal. Jim laughed at movies and videos that portrayed bigfoot as having clunky, loud, stomping strides. That just wasn't real.

They walked several yards into the woods and were completely surrounded by lush trees and bushes. The lights of the campground could barely penetrate to where they were standing. Jim's eyes were adjusting to the darkness, and he could see Charlie surveying their surroundings. He seemed to have better night vision than humans and never seemed bothered by the darkness. Right now, he was narrowing his eyes at something behind Jack. Jim strained his own eyes, but he couldn't see a thing. Finally, he could hear something moving through the brush toward them. Thinking it might be someone who would find Charlie, his heart clenched. He whipped his head around to tell Charlie to hide, but Charlie was already invisible in the brush behind them. Turning back to face whatever it was, Jim waited. Finally, a small rabbit hopped out of the darkness and into the soft glow of the light from Jack's phone.

"Just a rabbit," Jim laughed. Charlie appeared by his side again, just as quickly and silently as he had disappeared.

They walked quietly through the woods, with Charlie leading the way. He could see snakes and other dangerous things better than Jack and Jim, so he was their guide. They let him take them all the way around the perimeter of the stand of woods that separated the campground from the main road. On one side, there was a barbed wire fence that separated them from private property. The walk allowed Charlie to stretch his legs, and it made Jim sleepy.

"Ready for bed? I'm pretty tired," he told his dad. Charlie looked at him with concern. He looked tired to Jim but equally excited.

"Let's get back. We have to be up early tomorrow anyway."

They got back and Jilly was already passed out on her little bed. Jim looked at her and had to laugh. Her arms were flung over her head, which was hanging off the edge of the bed, her mouth was hanging open, and her left leg was bent with the foot on the wall.

"Hey, guys," Karen said. She was getting things cleaned up and ready for bed. "You need to get to sleep. You have an early day." She smiled at Charlie. "Maybe we can find out about your family, huh?"

Charlie didn't understand what she was saying, but he smiled at her kindness while Jim helped him get his bed rolled out on the floor.

"Okay, you two, we're going to sleep. You better get to sleep right away." With that, she and Jack disappeared in the back bedroom.

Jim started to climb over Charlie to get to his bed, but Charlie grabbed him and effortlessly hoisted him up on the bed. He sat there for a moment, looking at Jim with a small smile on his face. He reached out and patted Jim on the head.

"Charlie, I'm going to try to find out about your family tomorrow. I hope I find them for you." He reached out and patted Charlie's head in return.

Charlie bent low, and Jim could hear him getting settled on the floor. The whole RV shook with his large movements.

Jim was so tired that he barely had time to think about his day tomorrow before he fell into a deep sleep.

CHAPTER FIVE
Signs

AFTER WHAT SEEMED like just a few minutes to Jim, his eyes popped open, and he realized that he was feeling the RV rock. Charlie was up and following Jack outside.

"Where are you going?" Jim asked.

"Oh hey," Jack said, his voice a whisper because Jilly was still sleeping. "We're heading out so Charlie can have a little outing before the day."

"What time is it?" He rubbed his eyes, trying to clear away the drowsiness.

"Just before six. Your mom's going to make some breakfast."

"Okay." Jim rolled out of the bed and dropped down to the floor. Karen was already up and moving around the kitchen area.

"Hey, Mom."

"Hey, doll. What do you want to eat? I have frozen waffles." She was shaking the box enticingly.

"That sounds good." Jim loved sweet waffles. He trudged to the bathroom, still feeling half-asleep. His legs felt wobbly and heavy with the remnants of his slumber.

He and his mom got the breakfast stuff together, and he got ready for the day. When Jack and Charlie returned, they ate and talked about the upcoming events. Jack and Jim would do their best to find out about any of Charlie's family in the area. Unfortunately, this meant that Charlie, Karen, and Jilly would have to stay put in the RV for a good while, with little, careful outings. Jim felt bad for them, especially Charlie, but he knew that they were doing their best.

When it was time, Jim went to Charlie and grabbed his hand. "Charlie, we're going to leave you for a little while, but we're trying to find your family. I promise I'll do my best to find them for you."

Charlie smiled and squeezed Jim's hand. He understood that Jim and his family were trying to help him. He nodded at Jim, and Jack called Jim to go.

Jim hopped out the door and called back in to his mom. "Bye, Mom! I'll text you what's going on!"

"Okay! Be careful!"

They got in their Jeep and slowly drove through the campground. There were plenty of people awake and moving around outside now. Jim had noticed that camping people tended to wake up early.

When they reached the main road, there were no cars to be seen in either direction. Jim figured it was still a bit early for everyone to be heading to work. As they passed Mel's, they saw quite a few cars in the lot. There were plenty of people there, getting breakfast before work. Jim wondered if many of the people who lived here actually cooked for themselves. Laughing at his thought of a bunch of empty, unused kitchens, Jim started thinking about living in a place like this. He could see pros and cons. Maybe having a secret as big as Charlie made the idea unpleasant.

Before he knew it, they were pulling up to the gate of Hoke Farm. It was open now, and they could see tire tracks in the morning dew. The crew was already there.

"Well, here we go," Jack said. He gave Jim a look that was somewhere between excitement and dread. "Hopefully these people aren't too annoying, huh?"

Jim laughed.

They drove down the winding driveway and watched the old farm house grow larger. It was magnificent. The house had a stately feel to it, Jim thought. He noticed that it was a lot bigger than he had even realized. There were a couple of smaller buildings to either side of it and at least four fireplaces, because he could see four chimneys. Jim wanted to see inside. There was a fun-looking set of stairs on the outside to reach the upper balcony. The paint was fresh white with dark green trim. Jim liked it.

"Dad, this is really cool. Think we can go inside?"

Jack looked at his son. Like Jim, he liked historical places and probably wanted to go investigate nearly as much as he did. "Not sure. We'll see. I read that the house is over a hundred years old and housed four generations of the Hoke family. Mr. Hoke was one of the founders of this town."

"Cool."

They pulled around the back and saw the van. The crew was waiting for them on the back porch of the house. They could also see a large barn out back. Jack parked, and they got out to join the crew.

"Hey, there! Didn't chicken out, eh?" Pete was grinning in a rather slack-jawed way that was annoying to Jim this early in the morning. *Maybe this was a bad idea*, he thought. *Or maybe I'm just being too grumpy.*

"Course not. We'll see if there's anything to worry about anyway," Jim said.

Pete laughed and Shawna smirked.

"Not a true believer, are we?" she asked.

"I don't not believe. I just want proof."

"Don't we all?" She brushed her hair back and started gathering more equipment.

Larry was looking through a binder of some sort, his eyes darting between the pages, then to Jim, then to Shawna, and back. He slowly sidled over to Jack, but he seemed scared of him. His body was angled away, and he was reluctant to look at him. Jim thought he was really weird.

"Hi, I'm Shawna." Jim turned to see Shawna move forward with large strides and put her hand out to Jack. Larry looked relieved that he didn't have to interact with him yet.

"Jack Thomas. Nice to meet you."

She smiled. "Your son's quite a guy. He'll be a good addition to this episode. Would you like to follow along? We can have you follow, but you'll have to stay out of the camera's path. Just keep close to Larry."

"Sure. Thanks for letting us be involved."

She turned to Larry and barked out, "Larry, get him the form." To Jack, "We have a standard liability release form that we need you to sign. For both of you. We don't anticipate any problems, but you know."

"Sure." He looked at Jim and grinned.

"Where are we going?" Jim asked.

Shawna answered. "We're heading back in the northwest quadrant of the farm. It's closest to the river back there, and we think a squatch would need a good water source. There's also a creek on the east side. Yesterday we tried the southwest side because it's nearer to the farm and the rest of town. The neighbor over there has a vegetable garden. You know, an easy food source. And they claim to have seen it."

Jim knew about bigfoot and vegetables. Charlie got into trouble with the Whittles because he was crossing the lake to get to a vegetable garden. Thinking about this, he realized that it was more evidence that this was the place. There might be a bigfoot here.

"So what do bigfoot eat? Do they eat veggies, or meat, too?" Jim asked.

Jack looked at him with a twinkle in his eye. He looked close to laughing but somehow managed to reign it in.

"We believe they're omnivorous." She looked at him quickly. "You know, they eat both?"

"Yeah … I know what omnivorous means."

She looked sharply at him. "Smart kid." Her eyes quickly went back down to her pack that she was fidgeting with.

"Let's get going," Pete said as he ambled down the driveway toward the barn. He was carrying a camera and a bunch of packs. His vest was full of other gadgets and equipment.

Larry, on the other hand, had one small messenger-type bag slung over a shoulder and a sort of clipboard with a storage compartment full of papers. He was jotting down notes, his birdlike head moving quickly here and there.

Shawna moved forward and pushed past Pete, taking the lead. She walked with long, purposeful strides, her shoulders back and head held high. Jim thought she definitely looked like she should be on TV. She had such a strong personality.

Jack tapped Jim's shoulder.

"Hey, be on the lookout for any of Charlie's friends or family. Let's not let these guys ruin our mission, okay?"

"Okay, Dad."

"And don't let them make you do anything stupid or do anything stupid to you."

"Got it, Dad."

"I know, just wanted to re-enforce it." He smiled and turned back to the trio in front of them. "This is going to be a long day, but hopefully the opportunity they've provided proves useful."

"No kidding. I don't know how long I can stand them. You hear Shawna with that 'omnivorous means they eat both' thing?"

Jack laughed.

"I think you put her in her place, though."

"Yeah, well," Jim grumbled. He didn't like being treated like some stupid kid.

They walked to the barn and Shawna stopped, looking around. "This is a good spot. We'll do a first shot here."

Larry and Pete started moving quickly to set up for a shot. Larry found a good background and told Shawna a little bit of history about the place.

"Yeah, I remember from yesterday," she cut him off. Larry blinked and stepped back. She looked at Jim. "Hey, kid. Come on over. This will be your intro shot."

Jim suddenly felt embarrassed and shy. He never liked much attention, and this was too much. But he was doing it for Charlie. And Charlie's family. He took a deep breath and walked into the path of the camera.

"Okay. Stand there, and we're just going to be talking, okay? I'm going to look at the camera and introduce you a little bit, then ask you a few questions. Got it?" Shawna looked at Jim expectantly.

"Sure."

"You'll do great, Jim." She smiled at him. Her smile was radiant, and Jim actually saw a nice girl. Possibly. She had never called him Jim before, and he appreciated it.

"We ready?" she asked, looking at her crew.

"Ready," Pete said.

"We're good. In three, two, one," Larry counted down and pointed at Shawna and Jim.

"We're here at Hoke Farm again, and this time we're joined by our newest investigator and squatcher, Jim. He's been interested in bigfoot stories all his life, and now, in a turn of fate, he's met up with us in the perfect place to hopefully see his very first bigfoot."

Jim's eyes were drawn to a quick movement to his right. He saw Jack flinching and turning away really quickly. Jim knew he was laughing and wanted to laugh, too, but he held himself together. He was surprised at how Shawna was able to just throw out a lie like that. Well, an exaggeration. She had no idea if this had been a lifelong dream or not.

What she also didn't know was that Jim had Charlie. His best friend was a bigfoot, and this thought made Jim smile. He knew none of these goons had ever seen even the slightest trace of a bigfoot.

Shawna turned to Jim. "Jim, how are you feeling?"

Feeling slightly like a deer caught in headlights, Jim hoped his face wasn't turning red. "I'm very excited, Shawna. This is going to be great. I know you guys will be able to teach me a lot, and hopefully we'll see something."

Shawna gave him the slightest of nods and looked very pleased with his answer. From behind the camera, Pete gave him a thumbs up. Larry was looking only slightly less nervous.

"That's right! We're going to do our best to get whatever evidence there may be."

Shawna looked at Larry. "We done here?"

"Sure, Shawna. Looks good."

Jim had the idea that Larry didn't really have any control here.

"Okay. Good job, Jim. You were perfect. Just keep that up."

She turned with a flip of her hair and marched down the driveway. The others followed behind. Jim noticed that as they walked along, the driveway turned from gravel to dirt. It became a dirt path that wound through the woods, kind of like at his home. He started thinking back to last summer when he first found Charlie. He had been walking through woods like these and had seen and heard strange things. Hopefully they could hear and see some of the same things here.

His quiet reverie was interrupted when he noticed the others stopping. Shawna turned to Pete and Larry and asked, "This where we heard it coming from yesterday?"

Larry was examining notes on his clipboard. "Yep. This is it. About."

"All right, let's set up a shot here. We'll spend a little time listening, making some calls, whatever."

"What types of calls do you make?" Jim asked.

"Save those types of questions for camera," Shawna said as she checked her make-up in a small mirror.

They spent the next hour sitting and standing, alternately, making calls here and there. A couple of times, they recorded some interviews and questions to Jim. They heard nothing.

Jack was standing to the side, beside Larry, looking quite annoyed. Jim knew how he felt. "So is this what you guys do?" Jack asked once the camera was off.

"What we do? Yes, we investigate," Shawna answered.

"Yeah, dude! We investigate. You gotta be patient," Pete said.

Jack just looked at them.

"Why don't we move around? See if we can find any tracks?" Jim asked.

Shawna was looking somewhat miffed at them, but she said, "We're going to do that right now. Sometimes it's best to try to make vocal contact early on rather than tromp around making noise and scaring them away first." She pushed by both Jim and Jack and hurried off down the path.

They walked around for a while, keeping quiet and looking for signs. Larry had a map of the property to keep them on track, which he was now consulting while they took a short break. Jim was feeling like this was a bad idea. They were in the right place, but they were stuck with these people and not free to do what they needed to do.

He was thinking about all of this when he felt a nudge from Jack. Looking up, he saw his dad pointing slyly to his right. On the ground, three feet to the right of the path they were on, was something right out of a movie or TV show. It was just like in the pictures that people post online. It was a huge footprint in the soft dirt, next to a tree. Jim was struck by how silly it seemed in that moment, in that place. It was just so ... conspicuous and almost ordinary, since it looked like all those pictures. Looking more closely, he realized that most people would actually have seen it as just some type of imprint or dip in the dirt and not actually a footprint. It was hard to make out, but it was definitely a print.

He looked quickly up to Jack and then to the trio in front of him. They hadn't noticed despite their supposed professional big-foot hunting skills. He almost laughed. It seemed too easy to find, but maybe that was because they were used to seeing such things. Either way, Jim was glad they had seen it and the others had not. They looked at each other and nodded. They weren't going to say anything.

Jim's spine tingled. He was excited. This was proof now that there was a bigfoot in the area. It was just a matter of finding it. He only hoped the crew didn't find it. He wanted to find it in secret.

They walked on and finally made a long, winding, then loop-ing circle back to the house. Coming out on the other side, they could see beautiful ivy vines growing up on this side of the house.

Shawna turned to the group. "We'll break for lunch. Then we need to head back out and get some more shots."

"Well, we didn't see or hear anything, so I suppose so," Jim mumbled under his breath.

The crew had sandwiches they had picked up from the little store that doubled as a lunch counter. Jim loved his turkey and cheese. It was surprisingly delicious. He and Jack sat on the wrap-around porch in a couple of old rocking chairs, just listening to the sounds of nature. The cicadas were going strong, birds were chirping, and there was someone mowing grass fairly nearby.

Jack leaned in and said, "We need to come back here tonight. With Charlie."

"Yeah. This is going nowhere. They have no idea what they're doing."

Just as he said this, he looked over to see Pete pulling out some odd devices and setting them up on a folding table. He had some wood pieces, a recording device, some other cameras, food, and what looked like things to make plaster casts. There was also a very silly looking fake bigfoot that looked like it would hang from a tree, and a jar of some weird little orange plastic chips that resembled air fresheners. Stepping up to the table of items, Jim saw that the jar said "Sasquatch Pheromones" on it.

"What's that?" he asked Pete, pointing at the chips. He couldn't imagine how they got real bigfoot pheromones.

"That, my friend, is awesomeness. We have real primate and human pheromones that these suckers should be attracted to. Most people don't use them, but we're hoping to get some good feedback from 'em." He looked at Jim as though he should be thoroughly impressed.

"But what if they aren't the right pheromones?"

Pete's smile faltered slightly. "They are. Primates should be attracted to them and humans. Other animals have been attracted to them before."

"We're primates," he said. Pete looked at him blankly, so Jim pressed on, "But we don't know what a bigfoot is exactly, so how do we know it really will work?"

Now Pete's slack-jawed look returned. "Look, I don't know. People say it'll work, so hopefully it will." He turned his back to Jim and busied himself with the rest of the supplies.

Jim moved back to Jack and waited until Shawna came up and announced that it was time to go out again.

They spent time setting up cameras, bait, and those phero-mone chips, this time on the far east side of the farm. They put up a couple of the decoys, as well. Jim asked questions here and there, with prompting from Shawna or Larry. All in all, it was a very un-eventful afternoon.

After walking back to the Hoke house, they did one final in-terview with Jim. He had to ask questions and act enthusiastic about the possible results, while Shawna explained that they would be back the following morning to collect the items and go over the footage.

"Well, Jim, I hope you had a great time learning about our hunting techniques and are ready for some good results tomor-row," she said.

"I really did learn a lot about what you guys do, and I do hope we get something good on camera," Jim said as enthusiastically as possible without feeling too stupid.

Shawna looked at the camera and said, "We're done," then started walking off toward the porch. "You did great, kid. We'll have more tomorrow, same time. Then maybe tomorrow night. Night is usually a good time to investigate."

"Okay," Jim called after her.

Jack stepped forward. "You think you'll get anything?"

Shawna stopped and looked at him. "Hopefully. You never know. We usually get something interesting, though."

"Great. We'll see you tomorrow."

Jim followed Jack back to their car. He was exhausted but wired from the fact that there was definitely something out there. He wanted nothing more than to get Charlie and come right back, but they couldn't.

Jack spoke first. "We need to come back here. Tonight. With Charlie." He started up the car and turned around in the driveway. They started back to their campsite.

"I know. This could be it, Dad." He was too excited. His legs felt like they wouldn't stop moving as he sat for the short car ride back to the campsite.

When they pulled into their spot behind the RV, Jim jumped out and ran for the door. He sprang inside and yelled for Charlie. "I think we found one! There's one there!"

Charlie was sitting on the floor of the RV with Jilly while she drew some colorful pictures of what appeared to be cats. Of course they were cats. She always drew cats.

Karen's head snapped up at the loud intrusion. "What did you see?"

"A footprint. A big one," he answered with a wink.

She stood and looked at Charlie, then back to Jim, and then Jack as he entered. "What's the plan?"

Jack said, "I think we're going to go back tonight with Charlie. We need to be able to go look without intrusion, and the team is going tomorrow night."

"Okay."

Charlie was watching their interaction and looked like he could sense their excitement. His eyes were lighting up, and he looked inquisitive.

Jim bent down to see him. "Charlie, we may have found another one of you. We're taking you there tonight. This could be it!" He couldn't help grinning.

And Charlie began to grin, too.

CHAPTER SIX
Nighttime Mission

AFTER THE SUN went down, Jim, Jack, and Charlie got ready to leave for the farm. As they were stepping outside of the RV, Jilly pulled Jim aside. She looked up at him with her huge hazel eyes and smiled.

"Here, Jimmy. This is the picture I drew with Charlie's help. It's him and his family." Jim looked at the picture she had in her small hands and couldn't help but smile. She had drawn Charlie with his brother and sister, who she had named Buddy and Buttercup. Jim had no idea where she came up with those names.

"Great job, Jilly. I'll take it with me to show them when we meet them." He winked at her and hopped down the stairs.

They had to be careful about keeping Charlie from being seen as they entered the vehicle. Jack pulled the Jeep in sideways so that Charlie could crouch low, and he entered quickly through the side door. The tinted windows were enough to obscure Charlie a little as he sat in the back seat. He took up almost all of the available space back there and didn't look comfortable with his head bent forward, trying to shrink his frame out of sight. Without the tint on the windows, he would be failing.

Jack drove them to the farm and slowed. He killed the lights and pulled to the gate at the entrance. All three of them leaned forward and searched the sprawling acreage for any signs of people. After a few moments, Jim noticed his vision adjusting to the darkness, and he was able to see all the way to the farmhouse, thanks to the moonlight from above.

Nothing stirred.

Jim felt conspicuous just sitting there at the gate, but they didn't know where to go to secretly penetrate the farm. The gate that was unlocked previously was now locked. The crew must have been given the key for their time at the farm, or someone had let them in.

"Let's go farther down the road. This place has to have a back entrance," Jack suggested.

He backed out onto the road and headed farther down the small country road. They drove in silence, each looking for some sort of way in.

Finally, Jim saw it. There was a barely discernible opening in the thick brush lining the road. It appeared to have once been a nicely cleared path through the trees, but it had begun to grow wild again. Still, it was enough of an opening to drive through. Barely.

"Dad! There's a trail. Looks like it used to be a driveway of some kind," Jim said, pointing.

Jack stopped the car and squinted into the darkness. After a moment, he straightened with renewed energy. "I see it. It does look like an old driveway. Like the one we have at the end of road. Only thing is someone will be able to tell we drove in there once we do."

Jim was worried about someone finding them, but if they only stayed at night, nobody would know until morning. Still, if they wanted to be able to come back, they would have to cover their tracks.

"Maybe we can hide our tracks," he suggested.

"Let's pull in and see if we can find something to do that," Jack agreed.

They pulled in the rough former driveway and stopped just inside the trees. The canopy was so low now that it brushed along the top of their Jeep.

"Stay here, Charlie," Jim said, and he got out. Meeting with his dad at the back of the Jeep, Jim saw two ruts in the tall grass and weeds that had grown up in the driveway. He saw Jack looking upward. There were many branches from the trees on either side of the path. Jack then looked inside the brush a bit and started to smile.

"Look, there are some dead branches on the ground. Let's just pull those over here and hope they block any view of our tire tracks."

They worked quietly and quickly. Stepping back, they surveyed their work in the moonlight and were pleasantly surprised at the result. The tracks were mostly obscured. They stepped around the branches and got back in the Jeep. Charlie had been watching their progress, his torso wrenched around, leaning over the backs of the seats. His weight was bending them quite a bit. Jim noticed Charlie was taking in deep breaths, sniffing the air. His eyes were flashing excitedly. He seemed to sense something they couldn't.

"We're here, Charlie. I hope we can find something." Charlie looked back at him with his mouth parted and eyes shining.

They drove in silence again, slowly making their way through the thick grass and weeds and the encroaching tree branches. The once large driveway had become a green tunnel of wild growth. It was still large enough to allow the passage of their Jeep, but just barely.

Unsure of how far the driveway went and where it emerged, they stopped after only a few minutes of driving. Wherever they were, it was far enough from the road, and anything else, to be seen.

"Come on, Charlie," Jim said. He opened Charlie's door and tugged at his arm, anxious to get started.

"Let's be careful about this," Jack warned. "Let's listen carefully and take things slowly."

They took a few moments to listen and take in their surroundings. To their right, they could hear what sounded like water. They knew there was a creek that ran through the property. It had been on the map they had consulted in the RV after discovering the place. The rainfall earlier in the week had probably filled it enough that there was some running water along the way. It drained into a nearby lake. Hoke Farm was a large, fairly rectangular piece of land. The creek that ran through it actually formed the east end of the land and curved sharply west to form the northern barrier of the farm.

Jim heard a loud snuffing sound and looked at Charlie. He was standing tall and taking in a deep breath. His eyes were bright, and he seemed excited. Jim looked at Jack, and they shared a hopeful but cautious look. Jim wanted this to be it, but he didn't want to be disappointed if it turned out differently.

Charlie took a step forward and looked at Jim. It was like he was asking for permission.

"Go ahead, Charlie. Let's see what we can find," Jim encouraged.

He walked on with huge strides that only a bigfoot could take, and Jack and Jim had to keep a good pace in order to keep up with him. They didn't need lights yet, as the moonlight shone through the trees above and created a soft glow. The woods were alive with the sounds that only a deep, dark night can bring. The cicadas were nearly deafening, except that the guys were all so used to hearing them by now that the insects just created a background noise. There were crickets, tree frogs, bullfrogs, and what may have been alligators from the creek. Bugs of all sorts were out and about, especially lightning bugs. Balls of green light flickered here and there, giving the woods a mystical feeling to Jim.

Charlie stopped here and there, listening intently and sniffing the air. He walked as if he was tracking something—moving forward, pausing, getting his bearings, and moving forward again. Jim didn't want to break Charlie's focus or pull his attention away from whatever he was tracking. He just followed as closely behind as he could and tried his hardest to hear or see whatever Charlie was hearing or seeing. His senses just weren't acute enough.

They walked on for half an hour before Charlie stopped for more than a minute. Jim stepped to his right and studied his face. He appeared tense and ready for an encounter. His expression was that of confusion rather than excitement. He sniffed the air repeatedly. Finally, he looked down at Jim, and Jim didn't like what he saw. While he had expected excitement, maybe some apprehension, what he hadn't expected was fear. Jim's stomach tightened, and he was about to ask Jack what he thought was wrong, when Charlie held up a massive hand.

Just then, there was a loud screeching sound that Jim had never heard before. It was something between animal and human. It didn't sound friendly and sent a tingle down Jim's spine. He looked at Charlie and saw that he had tensed up and, again, was listening hard.

Jack whispered behind them, "Is that what I think it is and is it a friendly?"

Jim couldn't answer. He was sure it was a bigfoot, but he didn't know why it was screaming, unless it was scared. Still, he was frightened.

"Charlie? What is it?" Jim asked. After a few seconds, Charlie finally lowered his gaze to Jim. His eyes held apprehension and … something else. It looked like curiosity and excitement. Jim felt a little better seeing that Charlie wasn't as scared as he felt. He started to motion that they should go forward, but Charlie put out a huge hand and stopped him. He then pointed a large finger at himself and then pointed forward. Then he pointed at Jim and Jack, then at the ground.

He wanted to go alone.

Jack stepped forward and shook his head. "No, we should stick together. We don't know who or what that is." Charlie looked blank at first. He didn't know what Jack was saying, but he could hear the tone of his voice and knew there was concern.

He patted Jack on the shoulder with a small smile, and then he put his hand on his chest. The look in his eye told both Jim and Jack that he could take care of himself. Jack looked at Jim and nodded.

They were going to wait for Charlie.

Jim looked up at Charlie and nodded his agreement, as hard as it was for him. Charlie then turned and walked away from them. Jim could see the moonlight glinting off the hair on his head and back for several feet before he completely disappeared behind a stand of trees.

He felt his stomach clench. He was worried about Charlie.

"Well, I guess we just wait," Jack said. He turned on his flashlight and moved to the side of the path. He bent down, looked at a large branch that had fallen, and sat down. "No snakes," he said with a smile.

Jim walked over and sat beside him. He felt really helpless and anxious right now, but there was nothing he could do.

They waited quietly, with very little conversation, for the better part of an hour. At one point, a loud noise turned out to be a rabbit hopping through the brush. Even the smallest animals can make big sounds in the woods. Finally, they started to hear some strange noises. First, there was knocking. It was like someone was hitting a stick against a tree or some other piece of wood. Then came the hoots and hollers. These were enough to make your hair stand on end.

This went on for half an hour. Jim and Jack could only sit there, listening, hoping that Charlie would be okay. Hoping that they would be okay.

It started to sound like things were winding down, when there was a sudden yell. Both Jim and Jack shot upright. More sounds floated to them. These were grunts, yells, hoots, screeches. The scary thing was that there were two definite beings making these sounds, not just one, and neither of them human. They looked at each other, but neither knew what was happening. Some of it had sounded like Charlie. Jim's mind quickly went through different scenarios, but none of them were good. He wanted to go to Charlie and help him.

"Dad, what should we do?"

"I don't know. I don't think we can do anything," Jack said. His eyes were wide. He looked unsure of himself. Jim had never seen his dad unsure of what to do.

They stood, wavering with indecision, until the sounds quieted. Jim wondered if anyone from the town could hear what they had heard. *Of course they could.* More than anything, he wanted to see Charlie—right now.

They didn't have to wait long before they heard something moving down the path before them. It was moving quietly, but they could still hear it. Jim was scared that it wasn't Charlie. His dad had bought him a knife for his last birthday, and he got that out now. Both Jack and Jim lifted their flashlights, ready to turn them on as soon as whatever it was got close enough.

The sound stopped just out of reach of their flashlights and there was a long, tense silence before, "Jiiiim," was heard from the darkness.

"Charlie! Are you okay?" Jim turned on his light and ran forward.

Charlie had an odd look on his face. He looked angry and surprised. Jim gasped. Charlie's lip was bleeding, and he had scratches on his face and hands.

"What happened, Charlie?" Jack asked. He was now examining Charlie's wounds. They didn't seem too bad, but they were still upsetting.

Charlie looked at Jim with understanding, but it looked like he didn't know how to relay to them what had happened. He seemed at a loss.

Remembering the picture he had grabbed, Jim reached into his pocket and unfolded the drawing Jilly had given him. He pushed it out to Charlie. "Is this who you saw?" he asked, pointing at Charlie's brother and sister.

Charlie looked at the drawing and then back to Jim. He shook his head. He pointed at himself and then put his hand a few inches over his own head. It was another like him, only bigger. Charlie's shoulders slumped, and his eyes dropped to the ground. He turned and began walking back in the direction of the Jeep.

Jack looked at Jim and said, "We'll find out more when we get back. We need to clean him up."

They walked in silence back to the Jeep and found a larger place to turn around. The drive back felt long to Jim. He was anxious to know what had happened.

Finally, they pulled into their spot by the RV and cautiously piled out. Once inside, Jim started. "What happened? Who was it?"

"Charlie! What happened?" Jilly squealed. She rushed to him and took his hand, her eyes full of concern.

"We think he ran into another bigfoot but not his family. Looks like they fought," Jim answered.

"Oh no," Karen said, turning around to go to the bathroom. Jim knew she was getting the First Aid kit they kept there.

"Charlie, what happened?" Jack asked.

They all knew Charlie was capable of more than anyone had imagined of a bigfoot, but this story was probably beyond his capabilities of telling them. He was looking around, sort of dazed. He probably hadn't seen another bigfoot in a very long time, maybe not at all, besides his family. Who knew?

Charlie grabbed the picture that Jim still held and just pointed at his siblings and shook his head. He repeated the gestures he had given them before, indicating a larger bigfoot. It was true. There was another bigfoot out there, and it wasn't his family. Just how many were in the world? Jim was thrilled with the idea of there being more than he had originally imagined, but he was apprehensive knowing that one had been so dangerous to Charlie.

That seemed to be all that they were going to get from Charlie for the night. He went outside to the tent and sat at the table. Jim followed him and sat beside him. They sat in silence and just kept each other company. After a while, Jim patted Charlie's shoulder. Charlie looked at Jim, and Jim could see appreciation and love in his eyes. Jim went inside where his parents were talking.

"Do you think we should leave?" Karen was asking.

Jack blew out a breath. "I think this was probably just an animal instinct. We should stay and find out more about this bigfoot. What if he has information that Charlie could use?"

"Like what?" Jim asked. His curiosity was piqued. What could Charlie learn from that jerk?

"Just think. They're more like animals than we are, right? This guy was scared. Charlie's big and a stranger. He was protecting himself, maybe a family. What if we let Charlie try again, if he wants, and see if he knows anything about Charlie's family? We can't just leave after finding another living bigfoot. This could be a great opportunity."

"I see what you're saying, Dad, but what about Charlie? What if this guy's still aiming to kill him?"

"We should trust Charlie. If he wants to do this, we should trust that he knows what he's doing."

Jim nodded his agreement.

Karen had been listening quietly and now said, "I think that's the best idea. I'm not sure I want Jim going out there again, though. Not with those people."

"Mom! I'll be okay. Dad will be with me, and we're in a group. Bigfoot don't come out and attack groups of people."

"How do we know? Until last year we didn't think they were real."

"We've never seen any stories like that. I promise, I'll be fine."

Karen looked at Jack, who had been listening to each side carefully.

He looked at his wife and said, "Karen, he's right. We'll be okay. We'll keep up appearances and hopefully get some more information."

She looked upset at first, then her face calmed, and she nodded. "Okay, I trust you guys."

Jim went to his mom and put an arm around her. She patted his waist.

Jack looked at Jim and said, "Let's find out what Charlie wants to do."

They went outside and found Charlie in the same place as Jim had left him.

"Charlie, do you want to go again?" Jack started. He was trying to mime the question to him, but it was looking like flailing to Jim. He got an image of those inflatable tube things they have outside of sales to draw people in and had to suppress a smile.

"Let me try," he said. He turned to Charlie and pulled out the picture Jilly had drawn, another piece of paper, and a pencil. He drew a stick figure bigfoot on the other page, because that's the best he could do, and pointed to it. Tapping it with the pencil, he said, "He's there," pointing away in the direction of the farm.

Charlie nodded. Jim then pointed at Charlie and to the picture again, then raised his arms in a questioning way. Charlie stared for a moment. Jim could see his mind working hard and thought that maybe he didn't understand, but Charlie then nodded again. He put his hand on his own chest, then on Jim's, and then on Jack's. He pointed away, toward the farm, and nodded.

They were going back.

CHAPTER SEVEN
Investigation

EXHAUSTED FROM THE day, Jim got ready for bed and fell into a troubled sleep. He dreamed about a massive, red-eyed bigfoot that was chasing him and his family. He woke with a start and remembered where he was. Thinking about his dream, he realized how stupid it was. That's not how they look, no matter how mean they are, and this one was probably just scared and being territorial. It was a stupid dream.

Jim shook his head and got out of bed. He looked down at Charlie's sleeping form. He was on his side, next to Jim's bed, snoring loudly. Jim smiled. The sky was turning blue, and his dad was already up, making coffee.

"Hey," Jack whispered. Jim looked at Jilly, her arms flung above her head. Nothing short of an earthquake would wake her. Charlie, on the other hand, was stirring. He had been a light sleeper at first, but since he had moved in with them, he had become more like Jilly. Jim imagined he felt safe and comfortable now.

"Hey, Dad. You sleep?" He stretched his arms over his head in a yawn. He was still tired because of his ridiculous dream.

"Yep. Ready for the day."

Jack was always able to sleep. Jim often teased him about his sleeping abilities, but he always marveled at them. After years in the medical field, Jack was able to fall asleep within what seemed like seconds upon laying down and function almost impossibly well on very little sleep. He could also wake up and be out the door, fully awake, within five minutes. Jim was not that way. Not yet.

Karen slept in this morning, so the guys were on their own with breakfast. They had some cereal and juice as they quietly talked about the day. Charlie woke up after a while and lay there, watching them converse. He looked curious and somewhat anxious. Jim could only imagine what he was feeling.

They got ready quickly and stepped outside the RV and into the tent. Charlie followed. They joined him on a short walk before they had to go. It was beginning to turn blue, and birds were waking up. Charlie walked beside them as they strolled silently, taking in their surroundings, each lost in their own thoughts. After a few minutes, Jim realized that Charlie had stopped. He was standing still, staring off in the woods. He didn't appear to actually be looking at anything. Jim could see how worried he was.

"Charlie," Jim said, walking back to him. "It'll be okay. We're going to find your family."

Charlie looked down at Jim. His eyes softened, and he put a hand on Jim's shoulder. The moment passed, and Charlie looked to be in better spirits. They walked back to the RV, and Charlie ducked inside. Jack and Jim got in the Jeep and headed to the farm.

It was another nice day, and everyone in town, again, seemed to be eating breakfast at Mel's. The roads were clear all the way to the farm. When they got there, the crew was just getting out of the van. Again, they took a long time getting things ready for the day. Shawna kept going over what they would do that day and what she and Jim would talk about. Jim felt like he was basically learning a script, with just a bit of freedom. Looking at the equipment, Jim was suddenly struck by how new and unused it looked. He didn't think they had been using it very long.

"Hey, where do you get your equipment? How do you pay for everything?" Jim asked Shawna.

She looked a bit perturbed at his questions. At first, she acted like she hadn't heard, but he persisted. Finally, she said, "Private donors help us out. They really believe in our cause and our abilities. They want to help us make it big. Make a difference," she added.

"Cool," he said as she walked away. He was wondering who these mysterious donors were, when he saw Pete scrutinizing him with a funny look on his face.

"What's up?" he asked him.

Pete sidled up to Jim with what had to be his version of a chuckle. It sort of crackled in a hoarse way. "Wanna know who these donors are?" His mouth was hanging open in a goofy, slack-jawed sort of grin. He either looked like a laid-back, fun-loving guy or a buffoon. Jim didn't know him well enough to figure that out. Pete clearly felt as if he had some great secret to share.

"Sure," Jim said, trying to put a little more distance between himself and Pete, whose breath was not the freshest.

That won't be good for attracting a bigfoot.

Pete made a dramatic show of looking all around them to make sure nobody else could hear. "Come here," he said, motioning him closer. Jim reluctantly leaned in. "Shawna's parents are loaded. Loaded. They buy her everything. She always wants to make it look like it's coming from other places, but it's not." He cackled lightly, looking over his shoulder to where Shawna was busy fixing her make-up.

Jim wasn't surprised. She seemed like she came from a nice family, and a lot of people have to finance their investigations themselves. Pete seemed to think this was something to laugh at, but Jim didn't care. He left Pete to his preparations and found his dad. Jack was sitting on the porch of the big house. His knees were bouncing; he looked anxious.

"What's up, Dad?"

"Just ready to get going. Now that we know there's one out there, I wish we weren't stuck with these guys. But I guess it's okay. We may be able to find out other information through them, and it gets us out here. We know what to look for."

"Yeah, it'll be okay." Jim felt stuck, too. They hadn't needed the crew so far, and it felt like such a waste of time.

Shawna's voice broke the morning quiet. "Let's go!" She had shouldered her pack and started walking down the driveway toward the woods. She was all business.

Jim and Jack followed silently, keeping vigilant for more signs of a bigfoot. They walked until Shawna stopped ahead of them. They were heading toward the stream on the far east side of the farm. This was close to where Jim, Jack, and Charlie had been the night before. Jim felt a tingle go down his spine while thinking about what had happened between Charlie and this mystery big-foot. He wanted to know who this bigfoot was and if it knew any-thing about Charlie's family. Were they that sophisticated? Were they able to communicate something so complex as that?

Shawna's voice broke through his thoughts. "Let's set up for a shot here. We're going to talk about the cameras we set up yester-day and set up some more that we'll continue to run through the night. We'll come back here tonight and record some investigating. Jim, you come here and just keep doing what you've been doing. It's been great. Ask questions!"

"Okay," Jim said. He knew she wanted him to ask questions so she could provide her "expert" answers.

She started out discussing the traps and devices they had left the day before and how they would collect them and analyze the data later. They did check the one tape trap they had set up. This one was just heavy duty tape wrapped around a tree trunk, sticky side out. They had put it in a spot where they thought that a big-foot might have to walk through and brush by the trees. The hope was to collect some hair for DNA analysis. Shawna walked up to the trap and motioned Jim to follow while Pete was recording.

"Let's see what we've got here. Hopefully we will have collected something." She strode up to the tree and made a show of studying it. "Here, Jim, come see what we've got."

"We got something?" He was somewhat incredulous. It seemed liked a long-shot that a bigfoot would actually rub against these particular trees. They had chosen the trees for their proximity to the trail and the fact that they led to a clearing and a stream farther away.

Jim walked forward and peered closely at the tape. He could see what could have been some animal hairs. There were only a few, and they did not look like Charlie's hair. To Jim, they looked to be from a squirrel tail or something like that.

Pete came forward with the camera. Jim moved aside, but Shawna moved him closer to her so that Pete could get them both in the corner of the shot. She was deft in her movements so that it wouldn't be noticeable.

"See here, Jim? Looks like some sort of hair. What do you think?"

Jim swallowed. He didn't want to lie, but he knew they wouldn't like his answer. Still, she had asked …

"Looks like squirrel. See the speckled pattern?"

Shawna looked at him sharply for a moment but quickly recovered. "I'd say you're right. See, we aren't quick to make something out of nothing. We want the truth." She reached into her bag and pulled out gloves, scissors, and a plastic bag. "We're still going to collect this evidence and log it, just in case."

Jim watched her meticulously cut away the tape and place it in the bag. He was somewhat impressed with her attitude and skills. Too bad it was all for a squirrel.

Shawna led the group through the woods to all the places they had set up traps, cameras, and other ploys. She pointed things out and talked to the camera all the way, with Jim jumping in here and there.

They were walking to the place where they had set up a camera the day before, when Jim heard the sound of water again. They were near the place they had encountered the mystery bigfoot the night before. Jim looked at Jack and saw realization in his eyes, too. He started looking around for any signs of the bigfoot. He noticed nothing. Shawna was talking about another investigation they had done and some sort of sound they had heard. Jim wasn't really listening.

"It sounded like a howl, something between an animal and a man yelling. We were debating what it was when we heard some knocking sounds. As we've said before, they're known to knock on wood or use wood to knock on other wood and communi—"

She was cut off by a strange gurgling sound that was louder than any gurgling sound Jim had ever heard. It almost sounded like a stomach gurgling, but there was an extra element to it. His brain was having trouble making sense of what he had heard, when he remembered his mother and sister's description of what they had heard when they saw Charlie for the first time.

It was a gurgling sound.

CHAPTER EIGHT
Close Encounter

JIM'S SPINE TINGLED, and he looked around himself. He saw nothing and tried to get his dad's attention. Jack was apparently on the same page, because his eyes were narrowed, and he was searching the woods to the left of where Jim and Shawna stood. Shawna, he saw, was frozen in place, with her face stuck between uncertainty and fear. Her brow was furrowed in confusion, but her eyes were wide and shining with a multitude of simultaneous thoughts, all sure to be wrong. Jim knew what that was like. He remembered not knowing what it was he was either seeing or hearing, but something inside reacts instinctively to the unknown and produces chills of fear.

He, on the other hand, knew exactly what was happening and knew that fear was very warranted. Jim looked at Jack, and they moved closer together. Jack's jaw was clenched, and his eyes were darting around on high alert.

"What was that?" Shawna asked. She had found her voice again and looked into the camera. Jim was silently laughing at the cliched "What was that?" question that people on all of these types of reality shows tend to yell out for effect.

Jim sensed movement behind him and turned to see Larry edging backwards. For a team who supposedly did this all the time, they didn't seem too familiar with strange occurrences in the woods.

"Now, bigfoot are known to make gurgling noises here and there," Shawna said. She was keeping her composure and actually continuing with the show. Jim was impressed. "Some think it's what their language sounds like. Perhaps there's one nearby, trying to communicate. Let's be quiet and see if we can hear something else."

Jim stood with the group, listening hard. He heard some distinct noises farther away than he had thought the gurgling had come from, but he may have been mistaken about the distances. He thought the noises sounded like something moving through the woods in a sort of semi-circle around their position. It was a little creepy to him, knowing that there was a bigfoot out there that had attacked Charlie. He had to remind himself that this bigfoot felt threatened and was territorial.

Shawna turned to him and began speaking again. "We can try some vocalizations to try to provoke some more communication. What we do is play some sound recordings that we know are friendly calls, and we can do some wood knocking."

Jim wondered just how they knew that those calls were friendly. He didn't want to mess with this bigfoot, but he knew they were stuck with the team and couldn't act suspicious by not following along. Shawna pulled out an audio recorder and began playing clips of recordings they believed were bigfoot. He thought the first was definitely a wolf, and the second he couldn't identify. The third sound made the hair on his arms stand up. It was the whooping sound he had heard Charlie make when he had first discovered him.

"Hey, that's a bigfoot," he said without thinking. Shawna's dark eyes flicked to his face, and he saw confusion and amusement in her eyes. She didn't say anything.

After a moment of silence, they heard a sharp whoop coming from way too close. It sounded as though the bigfoot was right inside a thick stand of trees that was directly ahead of where they were looking. Jim was nervous. Who knew what this one might do? He looked at Shawna and saw that her eyes were wide. She looked like a deer in headlights, her mouth even slightly parted in disbelief.

When she spoke, her voice sounded higher than usual, even in a whisper. "This is very exciting. The sounds we're hearing are just like those described by others who have encountered sasquatch, and just like any audio recordings I've heard. Let's listen again."

Jim looked at Jack, who gave him a reassuring nod. They stayed quiet for a few minutes, hoping to hear more sounds, with Shawna making whispered comments here and there. Nothing more was heard. Finally, Shawna called for them to move on. As they began walking along the path, toward the source of the sound, Jim could smell a faint odor. It was pungent, and he could tell that it had been worse at one time. It smelled like wet dog, mixed with sweat, dirt, and who knew what else.

It was the bigfoot.

Shawna began looking around as if searching for the source of the smell, her head twisting wildly on her slim neck. Jim heard Pete behind him say, "Dude, something reeks."

Shawna answered him. "It's exactly the smell that anyone who has encountered sasquatch describes. This is amazing. Jim, come get a whiff of this, we're really lucky to be experiencing this."

Jim automatically stepped forward and had no idea why. Shawna had a commanding presence. It didn't hurt that she was pretty, too.

She put an arm around his shoulder and pointed into the woods beyond. "I think it's coming from over there. Can you see anything? I can't see anything, but I sure can smell it. Tell me what you're smelling."

Jim felt himself turning red. He didn't like being the focus of attention, and she was so excited. "It smells like a really dirty animal of some sort. It smells like something that would make your eyes water if you were close enough." He remembered when he first smelled that odor and how shocking it had been. She really had no idea.

Shawna nodded enthusiastically. Her eyes were opened wide, searching for any trace of the source of the smell and noises.

They stayed there for quite a while longer, but there was nothing more, so they moved on. The rest of the morning was spent collecting the rest of their cameras and other supplies.

They trekked back to the main house, where Jim and Jack were released for the day and told to return by eight that evening. Until then, the team was going to go over some of the footage and audio recordings back at their bed and breakfast.

"Whoa, I'm glad to be out of there. Did you see how excited they got? I thought they had experienced that before. Some professionals they are," Jim mocked. The team's faces betrayed the fact that they had never before encountered an actual bigfoot.

"Yeah, that was almost funny, but I was a bit worried about what this bigfoot might do. He's a bit unpredictable, so we should be careful. Let's get back and get Charlie. We have to move quickly if we want to fit everything in."

After a bite of lunch and a nap, Jim and Jack were ready to go back to Hoke Farm with Charlie. They were going to risk returning in the day time, but they had noticed that not many cars went by the farm, since it was at the edge of town and the newer parts of town were busiest. Most people worked in these newer parts of town or took the road west to a larger city.

The drive there was uneventful except for the fact that Charlie had to scrunch down in the back seat in case anyone saw inside the

Jeep. He looked uncomfortable but anxious to get there. They quickly made it to their secret entrance and drove inside. They got out and took a second to listen. Jim smelled something sweet in the air. He hadn't noticed it before, but it smelled like honeysuckle. It was calming. He looked at Charlie, who was sniffing the air as well. Charlie seemed invigorated and had a determined gleam in his eyes.

They walked forward, Charlie leading the way. This time, he didn't hold them back. They trooped together, nobody speaking, everybody listening, on high alert. Before long, Jim found himself relaxing and enjoying his surroundings. These woods reminded him of home and when he met Charlie, but there was a difference. The underbrush was less dense, and he figured that was because there had always been cows grazing on the property. They took care of much of the young growth and had allowed the trees to grow tall, without a lot of brush underneath. Since the farm was no longer a working farm, there was a bit of growth beginning. He could see a good distance into the trees from where he was now. And he saw nothing unusual.

His mind was wandering to food—specifically on the ribs he would be ordering that night from the diner—when Charlie stopped. Jim heard him take a big inhale of breath. He was smelling the air. Something was near. Charlie put up his hand to Jim and Jack in a firm gesture. They were to stay behind for now.

Jim hated this part. He wanted to help Charlie and hated not knowing things. He and Jack sat down with their backs against a couple of trees. Neither was in a talking mood. After only a few minutes, they began to hear sounds. They were odd sounds that almost reminded Jim of an argument, but they were definitely not words. The sounds ended, and a few minutes went by. Finally, Jim spotted Charlie making his way through the woods back to them.

Both Jim and Jack stood up expectantly. Charlie trudged up to them with a shocked look on his face.

"What happened?" Jim asked immediately. His eyes were taking a quick survey of Charlie, looking for any wounds. He looked okay.

Charlie just looked back and forth between the two. He looked like he was thinking hard about what had just happened, but Jim wanted to know what had happened. Patience was not coming to him right now.

Charlie's head jerked up, and he turned around. They stood still, looking in the direction of where Charlie had come. Finally, Jim could hear what Charlie must have heard before. There was the sound of something moving through the woods toward them. Jim held his breath. He realized he was really excited to see another bigfoot, but he still didn't know what had come of Charlie's visit.

A hairy figure became visible through the brush. It had to be at least seven feet tall, and it was massive. Charlie was definitely a young adult rather than full-grown. The figure came slowly, with a lumbering gait. As it approached, Jim realized he hadn't taken a breath in too long. He emptied his full lungs and greedily sucked in fresh air. Charlie glanced at him with concern, but Jim waved him off.

The bigfoot came forward in the afternoon sunlight that was peeking through the thick canopy above, giving his hair a dappled appearance. Its fur was darker than Charlie's, and Jim could see some lighter patches. Jim got the distinct impression it was a male. It walked forward until it was about twenty feet from the trio and stopped. Charlie stepped forward, in front of Jim and Jack, and the bigfoot stayed where it was. Its face was more worn and gnarly than Charlie's. There were scars on its right cheek, and when it opened its mouth for a particularly deep inhale of breath, Jim could see its yellow teeth. It had a snarl on its face, and its eyes were hard. The thing looked mean.

It sniffed the air, probably smelling Jim and Jack, then let out a low growl. Charlie immediately stepped forward, his neck stretched out, chest puffed up. He made a strange noise that Jim had never heard before. It was a cross between a gurgle and a growl. The other bigfoot's eyes flashed, and its nostrils flared, but it seemed to back down. Its eyes took on a more curious look. Charlie's body relaxed.

"Charlie, who is this?" Jack asked.

Charlie turned to both of them and pointed over his shoulder, with a thumb, back at the other bigfoot. He patted himself on the chest. Jim got the feeling he was telling them that the new bigfoot was like him. Charlie then motioned to himself and the bigfoot, and he did some hand gesture that Jim couldn't understand. It was just a lot of flailing to him.

"What? You are going to talk?"

Charlie just looked at him. He then turned and started walking back to the bigfoot.

"Charlie, wait!" Jim was worried. Where was he going?

Charlie stopped and turned around to face Jim. His eyes softened and a smile crept to his face. He made a soft sound, almost like a purring growl. He walked back and patted Jim's shoulder. Jim was worried that he might be saying goodbye, but then Charlie pointed to himself, then back at Jim and Jack, one by one. He locked his hands together and gave them a firm shake. This was the sign Jim had been using for family. He nodded firmly. Charlie pointed up at the sky, then the ground where they stood, smiled, and walked away. Jim knew he was going to spend the night here, and they would get him back tomorrow.

Reluctantly, Jim and Jack watched Charlie and the new bigfoot disappear into the woods. Jim felt his stomach sink. Would he ever see him again? Of course he would …

They turned and began a quiet walk back to their Jeep. Tonight would be the longest night of Jim's life. He would have to walk through these woods with the TV crew, knowing that Charlie was still in there with some unknown bigfoot. He wouldn't be home and safe. He would be out there.

"Do you think he'll be okay?" Jim asked Jack.

"Sure. He'll be just fine." Jack replied, but his voice sounded less sure than his words.

"We'll get him back, right?"

"Of course. He's our family now." Jack looked down at Jim and smiled. His eyes weren't smiling. They carried worry.

Jim felt heaviness all the way back to the campsite. Only when they arrived did he realize they would have to explain Charlie's absence to his little sister and mother. Jilly would be especially worried.

When they entered, Jilly and Karen were at the dinette table playing some sort of board game. Both looked up and watched them enter, their eyes narrowing when Charlie didn't follow them in.

Jilly jumped up. "Where's Charlie?"

Jack answered. "He met the other bigfoot. He's staying with him to talk to him. I guess to get information about more of his kind, maybe about his own family."

"But he has to come back! Why did you let him stay alone? What if the other bigfoot hurts him? Charlie's my best friend!"

"Jilly, it'll be okay. He let us know that he would be back tomorrow and that he would be okay. We saw the other bigfoot, and he looked okay."

Jim noticed he left out the other bigfoot's grizzled appearance.

"Jimmy, do you think this is a good idea?" she demanded of Jim.

"I think Charlie knows what he's doing, and this is what he wants to do."

She looked hard at him for a moment. "Fine. But he better be okay."

Karen had been silent during the exchange, but she finally asked, "Do you think he might be happy here?"

"No! He has to stay with us!" Jilly shrieked. Her eyes were taking on a watery look.

"Honey, I know. We all love him. But if he has more of his kind here, maybe he would be happy with them. If—"

"But, Mom!"

"IF, he chooses to live with them, we should be happy that he'll have others like him and will be happy."

Jim felt like he was watching some lame movie about acceptance, but knew she was right.

"Yeah, if he can live with a family of bigfoot and would be happiest with that, he should," he said.

With that, the family fell silent, each left to their own thoughts of what might happen.

"Are you going back tonight, with the TV crew?" Karen asked.

"Yeah, we should. We'll be closer to Charlie that way," Jack said. He looked to Jim for agreement.

Jim nodded. He wanted to be close to Charlie.

The wait for the meeting time with the TV crew was excruciating for Jim. They had a light dinner, but nobody really had an appetite. Jim felt tired, but he couldn't nap. He found Karen outside and sat with her.

"Hey, honey. You doing okay?" She rubbed his back like she used to do when he was younger.

"I'm worried about Charlie. I guess I'm mostly worried about him leaving us," he admitted.

"I don't think he will. He loves the family, especially you and Jilly."

CHAPTER NINE
Dark Danger

THE TIME CAME for Jim and Jack to head back to the farm, and they were extra anxious to get there. Jim felt twitchy and noticed the same from his dad. They pulled into the farm and found the crew getting ready, as usual, under the light of the porch. Shawna and Pete greeted them and turned back to their preparation.

Within minutes, they were ready to go. Shawna spent a few minutes handing out flashlights and headlamps. She wanted Jim equipped with a mic, a headlamp, a walkie talkie, and he was given his own hand-held camera to carry. He had fun playing with the fancy camera for a minute. It was an infrared camera, so they could see things in the dark.

"Okay, so we're going in, and we'll do pretty much what we've been doing. I'll take the lead, as usual. I want to do some wood knocks again and play some recordings. We got some good results last time; hopefully we can repeat that. Ready? Let's go." She turned with a flip of her hair and was off.

Jim followed closely behind, making every effort to hear or see any signs of Charlie and his friend before they did. He didn't like being out there with them and just wanted to know that Charlie was okay.

Every few minutes, Shawna would stop to talk to them about what they were doing and share a story.

"The sounds we heard last night are exactly what a local farmer claims to have heard several months ago. He lives about half a mile down the main road and says that his whole family has heard that exact type of whooping sound that we heard this morning. They also have claims of hearing wood knocking, yells and screeches, and even a possible sighting. According to him, his son was riding a dirt bike on their property and came upon something large in his path. He was so scared that he crashed his bike, panicked, and tried to run at first, then found a tree to hide behind. His description of it was that it stood at least seven feet tall, lots of long, dark hair, and a very human-like stance and gait. He says that it watched him for a couple of minutes and then just turned and walked back into the woods on two legs, long arms swinging."

"Amazing," Jim said. It felt like the thing to say.

"Yeah, the kid was so scared he stayed hidden for ten minutes after the thing left and then got his bike and sped home as fast as possible."

"Did it ever threaten him?"

Shawna gave him a smirk. He caught it in the light of his headlamp. "No way. Bigfoot are known to be gentle creatures. There are stories here and there of them being threatening, but who knows how credible they are or if there was a reason for that behavior. It just seemed more curious than anything."

"That's cool."

Jim caught her pleased look in his camera. He panned the camera to the right and thought he saw a flash of eyes. He jerked the camera back to the spot, but they were gone, if they had even been there at all. A dip in the path nearly tripped him, and he realized he needed to be more alert to what he was doing. It was disorienting to walk while looking at the camera screen.

A sudden knocking sound brought his eyes up from his camera again. Shawna had stopped and pulled out two pieces of wood. She was striking them together repeatedly.

"What I'm doing now is called 'wood knocking,' and it's done to encourage a similar response from a bigfoot. They are known to use this technique for communication at long distances."

Jim almost laughed. He had never known Charlie to beat two sticks together or anything like that. Maybe others did, but he knew his bigfoot didn't do that. Then again, he had heard knocking when Charlie had met the other bigfoot. But he felt that was less about communicating with others and more about scaring any animals away.

A sudden screech made Jim freeze. It had been loud and it had been close. He looked at Shawna, who was frozen in place, too. Jim swung around to look at Jack and the others. Everyone was stunned. Jim was the first to react by grabbing Shawna and moving backwards. He brought her in line with his dad and the others.

"What was that? That was crazy," Shawna squeaked.

Jim took a look at the group, slightly illuminating them with his headlamp. Shawna had gone pale; Larry was swallowing constantly, his large Adam's apple moving up and down with each movement; Pete's jaw was slack and his eyes wide. In contrast, Jack's eyes were narrowed, his breathing was steady. He was ready for whatever was about to happen. Jim felt reassured by his strength.

Just when he thought the mysterious source of the sound had to have moved on, another screech pierced the heavy night air. This one sounded closer still. It was a creepy sound. Then the sound of something moving through the woods, toward them, from the left, began to grow louder. The TV crew all began creeping backward with unsteady steps. Pete nearly fell backward over his own feet, dropping his camera in the process. He made a loud "oomph" sound and barely caught himself before a loud growl came at them through the darkness, only this time it was to their right. All of the flashlights swung to the right, trying to pinpoint the source of the threatening sounds. Pete scrambled to pick up the camera and keep recording, while breathing raggedly.

Jim tried to train his camera on the spot where he had heard the sounds, but he saw nothing. He was very confused. He knew the sounds he was hearing were from the bigfoot, but he had no idea why he was hearing them. Charlie was with the bigfoot, so why was he coming after them?

Jack grabbed his shoulder, and Jim saw him point to the left. Jim probed that area with his own camera, which he made sure wasn't recording right now. In the ghostly gray display, he saw a flash of something moving through the trees. He searched the area again and found movement. He zoomed in and saw the face for only an instant, but it was enough. It was the face of the bigfoot they had found. He recognized it by the ragged scar. Instantly, he was worried about Charlie. It was strange that he had disappeared with this bigfoot and now here it was, threatening the group.

"This is amazing. We're hearing all sorts of sounds right now that are consistent with many reports of squatch encounters. I really hope the sounds are loud enough for the camera to pick up."

Shawna was back in host mode. She was trying to play this off as a great thing and safe, like the crew was in total control. Jim looked at her face and saw that her eyes were now gleaming. He couldn't believe it—she was excited. Most people would be running screaming through the woods by now. She had guts.

Jim heard crunching sticks and leaves ahead of them. It was moving back to the right. They were all following the sounds with their lights. Pete had stopped breathing, and an eerie silence crept over them. Jim was slightly anxious. To him, this was a different unknown. Rather than having never seen something like this before in his life, it was just like encountering a stranger who was acting oddly. He was curious and more worried about Charlie than anything.

A few seconds went by with no sounds except for the heavy breathing of Pete, and Larry's nervous swallowing. Jim thought the bigfoot had probably moved on. Maybe Charlie had convinced him to leave them alone.

A sharp snap of a stick to their right changed his mind. It was closer. Jim was suddenly aware of a whooshing sound. He thought it sounded like something cutting through the air, but he couldn't figure out what would be flying toward them. A huge thudding sound scared him enough that he jumped and his hands and feet tingled.

"Dude, what was that?" Pete yelled. His composure was slipping.

Jim realized something large and heavy had hit the ground a few feet to their left. Flashlights showed him that it was a very large rock. The bigfoot had thrown a rock at them. Was it trying to hurt them?

Another thud came from right in front of them, and they all jumped backward in order to keep the rolling, bouncing rock from hitting them.

It was trying to hurt them.

"It's trying to hit us!" Shawna hissed. "We need to get to a safer location."

That was all it took. They all turned and started scurrying as quickly as they could through the darkness. Panic was making them lose their way, and they had to backtrack once.

As they were trying to find the trail again, a blood-curdling screech sounded from right behind the group. They were all so instinctively scared that there wasn't even a second of frozen terror; they all immediately lurched forward, with Pete and Larry scrambling over one another. Shawna, Jim, and Jack were running in a more controlled manner, and each kept stealing glances over their shoulders.

Jack started to slow. "What do you—"

Another scream erupted from behind them. The group started to dart forward again, but Pete tripped and fell face-first into the ground. "Owww!" He started groaning and rolling on the ground.

Jim went back and shined his light in Pete's face. His nose was bloodied.

"My nose is broken! And I think I broke my wrist or something."

"Let me take a look," Jack said. He bent down and began examining Pete's injuries.

Jim noticed he and the others had subconsciously created a sort of perimeter around the two, with their backs to them, facing outward. He couldn't see anything or hear anything. His thoughts were racing. What was going on? What was Charlie doing? Was he involved? Was he hurt? Where was he? What was this bigfoot doing?

Scar's a good name for this guy.

"Ah, man. Watch it! That hurts." Pete wasn't being a good patient.

"Your nose is broken, but I don't think your wrist is," Jack concluded.

"I'm not running anymore. My face hurts too bad."

Larry finally spoke up. "I think we should get out of here as quickly as possible."

"Larry, this is big stuff. It's what we dreamed of! Let's not be too hasty," Shawna argued.

"Listen, Shawna, I ain't gonna get hurt over this," Pete said. He looked disgusted and miserable.

Jim heard Shawna grumble, "You're already hurt, you doofus. And it was your fault."

Jack looked around. "I think we should go back and regroup. I'm not sure what this thing is or what it wants, but it seems to not like us being here. We should at least go get Pete cleaned up and figure out what to do next."

Shawna started to argue, "This is the chance of a life—"

A screech cut her off. They all spun around, and the sight before them froze them all in place.

Scar was standing there at his full height, arms outstretched. He looked like a massive, hairy wall. His barrel chest was puffed out, and his eyes were shining in the glare of the flashlights, giving him a slightly demonic appearance. Jim was thoroughly terrified. He heard a curse word escape Pete's lips and Shawna gasped.

Larry, in a rare show of emotion other than nervousness, said, "We're all going to die."

"No, we're not," Jack said firmly. "Let's all move slowly back away from him."

He didn't have to tell them twice; they all began moving immediately.

Larry moved too quickly.

The bigfoot lurched toward him and swung a long arm. A human-like yell emphasized the threatening gesture. The yell was enough to make every hair stand on end. It was something halfway between a man's angry yell and maybe a giant ape-like howl. The bizarre, hard-to-define nature of it made it the most creepy thing Jim had ever heard.

Everyone scattered as he lurched after Larry. Somehow, Larry moved with lightning speed and was in front of the rest of the group before Jim had time to think about what was happening. They all turned and started running as fast as they could through the woods. Jim looked to his dad, who was running right beside him. Jack looked at him, his eyes narrowed. Jim could tell he was as confused as he was.

What had happened to Scar?

Jim and Jack were in the back of the pack. They were running behind the others, and Jim knew that was because the others were experiencing sheer terror, while they were mostly confused. Scar could have hurt them all if he had wanted, but he had obviously just been trying to scare them. Why?

They were in a particularly thick section of woods, with many trees that they had to dart around. Jim was zigzagging through a thick stand of trees, when he felt something grab his right shoulder and tug him off his feet. He let out a slight yelp and hoped his dad had heard, but he was too shocked to yell out for help.

His feet hit ground again, and he quickly turned to face his attacker.

CHAPTER TEN
A Family Affair

"CHARLIE!" HE YELLED before he realized he couldn't let the crew hear him. In a quieter voice, he asked, "What are you doing here? What's happening?"

Charlie gave him a big smile and a back-cracking hug. When he let him go, Jim saw him peer over Jim's shoulder toward the fleeing group. Jim turned off his light so that he would be hidden from them.

"Jim? Jim, where are you?" It was Jack. Apparently the sudden disappearance of his son had been quickly noticed.

"Over here, Dad!" He peeked out of the stand of trees and waved to his dad in the little bit of moonlight that was available. "Here!" he whispered loudly. The others were still running and pretty far away by now.

Jack moved quickly to him, and his face split into a grin when he saw Charlie. "Hey, boy! Where have you been?" They embraced, and Jim thought it looked really funny seeing these two big guys together, one hairy and one not. There was so much similarity yet so much difference.

Charlie looked at them both and gave them a wave to follow. Jim looked at Jack, who shrugged, and they began to trail after him. He took them through the same path they had followed and then left the trail and started blazing his own trail. It looked like he knew exactly where he was going, so Jim relaxed a bit and followed.

After many minutes, Charlie slowed. He was walking forward, tentatively, and looked like he was looking around for something. A low snuffing sound came from up ahead and to the left. Charlie made a similar sound and then more of a chuffing sound. Jim knew that he was communicating with Scar.

A figure suddenly appeared before them, where the sound had been coming from. Scar moved so silently that Jim hardly believed his eyes at first. He realized that the noises they had heard earlier were very purposeful. If a bigfoot didn't want to be heard, they weren't heard, so the breaking sticks and whooshing sounds of something moving through the woods earlier had been very intentional.

Charlie moved forward to greet Scar, and they began a low, gurgling conversation, complete with a lot of hand gestures. Scar grew louder and his tone more angry. Jim looked worriedly up at Jack, who put up a hand to tell him to be patient. Charlie listened patiently. When Scar was done, Charlie stood tall and began speaking firmly. Scar started to say something, but Charlie's tone rose, he shook his head no, and Scar quieted. Scar again began to get loud, and Charlie puffed his chest out and moved in close to Scar, his forehead against Scar's. He stared intimidatingly at Scar as he spoke in harsh tones. Scar stood for a moment, staring, then he turned his head. Charlie relaxed and spoke in lower tones. Scar finally nodded.

Charlie turned back to Jim and Jack. He smiled and gestured for them to come closer. They walked forward, while Scar studied them from the corner of his eyes. Jim finally got to see Scar up close.

He was more grizzled than he had even realized before. He looked like his life hadn't been easy. His eyes were shining, though. He was smart. Even with Scar, Jim could see something much more inside of this being than in other animals. He couldn't quite say human, but something close.

Charlie pointed at Scar and put a hand over his chest. He turned and looked at Scar, then pointed at Jim and said a very crude "Jim." He pointed at Jack and said what sounded like "Jim" again. Scar gave them an almost imperceptible nod. The introductions were over.

A small voice broke out over the ensuing silence. Everyone jumped. It took a few seconds for Jim to realize it was coming from the walkie talkie the TV crew had given him. He pulled it out of his pocket and heard Shawna's voice. "Hey, anyone there? Where are you guys? Are you okay?" Her voice was quavering and higher than usual.

Jim and Jack just looked at each other for a few seconds. Jim had forgotten all about them. *It's surprising how much you forget when a bigfoot is in front of you*, Jim thought. He held the walkie to his mouth and said, "We're okay. We got split up by the thing and a little lost. Where are you guys? Are you okay?" He looked at Jack and shook his head in an "I don't know" manner.

Shawna's voice barked back at them. "We're fine. We got a little turned around, too. We found the path, though, and we're heading back to the house. Can you make it back, or do we need to come find you after we regroup?"

"We'll be fine. We think we sort of know where we are," he answered. He shrugged at his dad, who nodded back at him encouragingly.

"Okay. We're going to get back to the house and help Pete out. He's pretty whiny right now. Keep in touch and get back as soon as you can. We need to do an interview about this." She sounded less worried and more excited.

"Got it." He stuffed the walkie back in his pocket and looked at Charlie.

Scar turned and gestured with his shoulder. They were to follow. Charlie walked in front of Jim and Jack, periodically checking on them over his hairy shoulder. They walked a long way through the thickest woods they had encountered yet. Scar was walking faster than they were, quickly creating a good distance between them. Jim was wondering just where they were going and what they were doing, but he trusted Charlie.

Finally, the grass and underbrush started looking more worn down. There was a lot of animal traffic all throughout this area. Jim looked up from inspecting the ground, and his breath caught in his chest. Scar had hurried ahead and was standing in front of what Jim realized was a little home. It was really well camouflaged so that if Jim had been walking by, he may not have noticed anything. However, looking closely, it was a thick stand of shrubs and trees, with added kudzu and other greenery to create an almost nest-like home.

But that wasn't what had stolen Jim's breath.

It was the three figures standing with Scar. There was a slightly smaller bigfoot standing next to him, and in front of them, with Scar's hand on its shoulder, was a juvenile bigfoot. The third figure was an infant bigfoot being cradled in the female's arms.

Scar had a family.

They were standing there, staring at the humans, with apprehension on their faces. The juvenile, who Jim saw was a male, moved behind his dad's legs and was peeking out at the strangers. Jim's jaw dropped. They looked like a human family, only different. It was shocking and amazing. He thought that after Charlie, nothing would shock him, but somehow this did.

Charlie had stopped and waved to the family, whose eyes flicked to him with recognition and acceptance but quickly returned to the humans. They weren't sure about this.

Jim looked at Jack, who had the same open-mouthed look that Jim knew he had, and said, "There have to be so many more all over the country, maybe the world."

Jack just nodded. His eyes were wide with awe, and they held a softness. Jim had never seen Jack so moved. Charlie watched them closely. He looked desperate for them to react a certain way. Jim thought he wanted acceptance, but he couldn't figure out why. Of course they would accept them with kindness.

"This is why the big one wanted all of us to leave. He has a family with a new baby. We're a threat to them," Jack pointed out.

All Jim could say was, "Yeah." He was staring and couldn't help it. A year ago, a bigfoot was just something that was fun to think about, but he hadn't thought it was actually real. Now, he had one living with him and was being introduced to a whole bigfoot family.

Jim looked up at Charlie, who was watching them intently. Jim smiled at him. He couldn't help it; this was unreal. Charlie grinned back and looked at Scar, who appeared to relax a bit. The rest of the family sensed the change and visibly relaxed, too.

Charlie walked over to the family and spoke with them. He turned and looked at Jim and Jack, then waved them over. Jim sprang forward. He hadn't realized he was so eager to see the others up close. They were fascinating. It was very clear to him, up close, that the mother was female. Her face was more rounded and feminine. Her body was more feminine, too. She had breasts and a difference in her hips and waist. The way she carried herself was very female. She just looked like a mother.

So Scar had a son! Jim was surprised at his youthful look. He had less hair on his face than the adults, and what hair he had was finer. His eyes were bright and curious. Jim liked him immediately. He thought that this is what Charlie had been like as a young bigfoot. Jilly would love him. He smiled at each of them in turn.

The mother looked apprehensive, but she was getting more comfortable with each passing minute. The boy was comfortable as soon as Jim had smiled. He took a step forward and looked at his dad. Scar stared for a moment, thinking. Jim could see it in his steely eyes. He finally gave a nearly imperceptible nod, and the boy sprang forward. He grabbed at Jim's clothes, his hands, he reached up for his face and hair. Jim laughed, and the boy froze. He cocked his head to the side and listened with a smile on his face. Unbelievably, he laughed, too. It sounded so human.

The boy turned his attention to Jack and began the same inspection of him. Jim watched in amazement. Charlie and the others were watching, their eyes sparkling with amusement. Jim turned his attention on the baby. It was a little larger than Jim thought a human baby of this age would be. It was hairy, but its hair was lighter and finer. Its face had a layer of peach fuzz on it. Every now and then, it would make a little cooing sound and take in a deep, contented breath.

Jack caught Jim's eye and said, "We need to get back. We don't want them coming to look for us."

"Yeah," Jim agreed. He didn't want to leave them just yet, but he knew they needed to get back.

They started to tell Charlie they would be leaving, and were backing away, when Scar stepped forward. He made a grunting noise and gestured forcefully at them and then began speaking to Charlie. Charlie listened, then put his hands up in a calming manner. He turned to Jim and Jack and pointed at the infant.

Jim looked at Jack, who shrugged, but they moved forward and looked more closely at the baby. There didn't appear to be anything remarkable about it. Maybe its skin looked a little red, but it seemed okay. Jim looked at the mother, who no longer looked worried about them. Her eyes were pleading with him. He looked back down at the baby and leaned in. There was something, a faint noise. It was a kind of wheezing sound. Suddenly, the little thing coughed.

It was sick.

"Dad, it's sick. I can hear a wheeze."

"Yeah, I see. They want help. Charlie must have told them we could help."

"Can we?"

Jack breathed out slowly. "I'm not sure. We can try." He looked at Charlie and said, "We'll help them. We have to go," he gestured away, "but we'll be back and try to help."

Charlie paused for a moment, as if trying to make sense of that, then nodded. He turned and spoke to the family. Their worried looks lessened slightly, and they nodded, too.

Jim and Jack began moving away with Charlie. "Charlie, we have to leave, and you stay here, but we'll be back later, with help," Jim tried to explain. He didn't know how to properly explain this with hand gestures, but he knew Charlie got the idea.

Charlie walked them back to the path, and they said goodbye. Jim hugged Charlie. He noticed that Charlie looked worried, but also somehow very happy, excited. Jim realized he liked being among other bigfoot. This made him worry. Would Charlie want to stay with them? What about his real family? What about his new family?

These questions gnawed at Jim as they hiked back down the path. They walked quickly back to the house and found the crew sitting on the porch, watching their footage.

They had found something.

CHAPTER ELEVEN
Care and Wait

THE AIR WAS buzzing with their excitement. Jim could feel it.

"Oh my God! Did you hear that? That's insane! We have the best audio anyone has ever had of a freakin' bigfoot!" Pete was on his feet, moving with the electric excitement that a close call brings. He looked like he couldn't be still.

"How did we not get any footage? This is ridiculous," Shawna growled. She was pushing the fast forward and rewind buttons furiously, searching for any sign of the thing they had encountered. Jim was pleased that they hadn't caught his image.

Larry was the first to spot Jim and Jack walking up the path. "Hey, you made it." His eyes were bugging out of his head, off and on, as he looked between the TV screen and the woods they had just come from. He was still nervous.

"Yeah. We got a little lost, but we made it back. Had to take it slow, while we made sure we weren't being followed," Jim said.

"You won't believe it, but we didn't get it on film," Shawna sounded exasperated.

"No way!" Jim feigned shock and disappointment. He knew they weren't used to being in situations like that, and they all had forgotten their cameras in their fear and desire to escape. He himself had turned his camera off and stuck it in the pocket of his cargo shorts when they had to run.

"Dude, where's your camera? I need it to go over the footage," Pete said, his hand out for the camera.

"Oh, here it is. I hope I got something good." He handed it over, knowing there was nothing of use.

"We need to be smart about this," Shawna said. She ran a hand through her hair. "Okay, we need to shoot me talking with Jim about this experience, then we all need to head back to our hotels or whatever and rest. We'll go over the footage ASAP, when we're not so excited. Too excited, we might miss something. So we won't meet here tomorrow morning. Okay?"

Everyone nodded in agreement. They went ahead with her plan, and Jim had to give an interview about what he had encountered. He tried his best to sound excited about it all, and he glossed over how long it took them to get back once they were separated. Nobody noticed anyway. They were too excited.

Once that was done, he and Jack excused themselves and quickly got out of there. It was a long ride back for Jim. He couldn't wait to tell his mom and sister about what had happened. They wouldn't believe it. Well, they would. After Charlie, anything's believable. But they would be excited.

When they pulled into their parking spot, Jim flew out and raced to the RV. He burst through the door, surprising Karen and Jilly. They had been sitting on the couch, watching TV, and both jumped at his intrusion.

"What's going on?" Karen demanded.

"You won't believe it. We found more of them! Charlie's with them now. Their baby's sick and they need help. We—"

"Wait a second, you found more? Did the TV crew see all of this? Did they see Charlie?"

Jack walked in during her questions. He closed the door and leaned against the sink, watching the proceedings with a slight smile on his face.

"No, of course not. We wouldn't have let that happen."

"We can't control everything, Jim," Jack interjected.

"I know, but we would try our best."

"We would."

"Okay, so anyway, we were out investigating and then all sorts of craziness started. There were sounds and howls coming from ahead of us. We could see things in the cameras. Oh yeah, they gave me an infrared camera to use so that we could see in the dark. So anyway, we get attacked by Scar! He came out of nowhere and chased us all back toward the house. Pete got hurt. His nose. Then we're running back, and Charlie gets our attention away from the group, so we split off. Then Scar and Charlie have this intense conversation. Charlie wins. You should have seen him! So we follow them to Scar's hiding place, home thing. He has a wife, a son, and a baby. The baby is sick, and they want help for it. We got back, and the crew didn't know what had happened, just that we got split up and lost."

He had finished his rambling and was pleased with the looks on Karen and Jilly's faces. They both had let their mouths fall open, and their eyes were wide.

Karen was the first to speak. "What's wrong with the baby?"

Jack answered. "Looked like a respiratory infection. I'm just guessing. It had a cough and kind of ragged breathing."

"I should take a look. Do you think something like that could take our kind of medication?"

"How should I know?"

Jim was, as usual, pleasantly surprised at how his mom jumped right on board with something so crazy and out of the ordinary.

"I'll get some things together. I guess we could try some things that aren't too dangerous. They're very similar to us …" She was thinking to herself now.

Jilly hadn't said a word. Jim realized how strange that was and turned his attention to her. She was busy digging through her bag at a frantic pace.

"Jilly, did you hear what we said?" he asked.

No answer. More frantic digging. Finally, she pulled out a baby doll. She carefully unwrapped the baby and pulled the little, pink blanket out, then folded it in a messy semi-square.

"I have a baby blanket for the new baby! Can we go see it?" Her eyes were shining.

Jim and Jack laughed. Karen smiled and said, "Aww, how sweet of you. I think your dad and I should go check on it. I'm not sure about how they would react to a bunch of us coming, and I don't want anything to happen to you guys."

Both kids erupted with complaints. Jim was loudest.

"Mom, that's not fair! I want to go." Jim was upset.

"Honey, you've seen them once, you've been going out there for days now, and I want you to watch your sister."

"This sucks. I'm not a little kid anymore."

"Jim! No more. This is how it has to be. We want to be careful about this."

Jim opened his mouth to argue again, but Jack held up his hand.

"Jim, you heard your mom. This isn't like you. I think we're both really tired from burning the candle at both ends for a couple of days in a row. Let's rest tonight. Your mom and I will go in the morning, and you can sleep in. Watch your sister. She needs you, too."

Jim was fuming mad. He knew he was being selfish and unreasonable right now, but he couldn't help himself. He had found himself opening his mouth before he had really thought about it. Right now, he did his best to nod and keep his mouth shut. He wouldn't get anywhere arguing. When he had been younger and tried to argue, his parents had always united and stood strong. There was no way that anger would win this one.

Jack was right. The two guys were beyond tired. They ate a quick dinner of sandwiches and fell into bed. It had been a long couple of days. And that was on top of traveling.

Jim fell into a deep sleep filled with dreams of Charlie and the others. In the dream, he was out of control and yelling at his mom. When he woke up, all he could remember was the awful feeling he had while he was yelling at her. In the dream, he had known it was wrong, that he was wrong, but he couldn't stop himself, no matter how hard he tried. It was terrible. He lay there, thinking about how bad it was and how it had just been an exaggeration of what had happened the night before. He would apologize to his parents as soon as he could.

His parents. Where were they?

He had suddenly realized how quiet it was. There was sunlight streaming in through the cracks around the windows. Birds were chirping their morning songs. He had forgotten all about them leaving in the morning. He sat upright and looked around. The sliding partition to their room was open, and the bed was empty.

They had left.

He must have been more tired than he had realized. Their departure hadn't disturbed his sleep at all. Jim slid his legs off his bed and sat there. He felt better now that he had had some sleep, but he felt like he should be there with Charlie and his parents. He had always been there. Jilly made a little noise and he looked at her. She hadn't gone with them at all since they got there. Her days were spent with Karen, either inside, around the RV park, or making short excursions into the town. Yet she hadn't complained at all. He felt pretty bad about the night before.

He got some breakfast and waited for Jilly to get up. They spent the morning lounging and watching TV. Jim looked at his phone every few minutes, checking the time and hoping for a message. He wanted to know what was going on.

Finally, at almost eleven, his parents pulled into the parking space. He anxiously waited for them to climb the steps of the RV, and when they entered, he peppered them with questions.

"Hang on. We'll tell you everything," Jack said. He walked to the refrigerator and got Karen and himself bottles of water. "We got there, and Charlie took us to the family. They were a bit scared at first, but they warmed up. Your mom checked the baby."

Karen had sat down on the couch next to Jilly. She looked stunned. "I still can't believe it. That was amazing. There are more than we could have imagined. The baby is going to be okay. She has a cough that apparently hasn't cleared up in a bit and wasn't eating well, so I gave her some antibiotics. A pedi dose. I hope there isn't a problem, but this antibiotic has been safe for all of our animals and us. She wasn't eating, so that made me go ahead and give it to her."

"I'm sure it'll be okay," Jack reassured.

"I hope so. This is uncharted territory."

"That's awesome. You're the first ever bigfoot nurse, Mom," Jim said.

She grinned at him, but he could still see worry in her eyes.

They ate lunch outside and quietly discussed what was going to happen. The baby would need a week's worth of antibiotics, and they wanted to monitor that.

So far, they hadn't heard from the TV crew. They were supposedly spending the first part of the day looking through their footage from the night before. Jim was anxious to hear what they got and hoped it wasn't much.

CHAPTER TWELVE
Subterfuge

IT WASN'T UNTIL late that afternoon that Jack got a call. The TV crew was thanking them for their time, but they wouldn't be needing them anymore. They were concluding their investigation and moving on. They thought this was weird but figured the crew was too scared to continue. Jim was slightly disappointed. He had liked hanging out with Shawna. She was cute and interesting. But he was glad that they could focus on why they were there in the first place.

Jim and his family were going to check on Charlie and the family that evening, since there was no TV crew to worry about. They would go just before dark. Jilly was so excited that she got out her nice dress to look really pretty when she met the new family. She spent the afternoon getting ready and drawing pictures that he suspected she wanted to present to them. She was also talking nonstop about Charlie, who she hadn't seen in a couple of days now. Jim felt bad. She had been left out for a while now, but she was taking it all so well. Her fiery, red-headed spirit had been politely subdued the whole trip.

Feeling pretty selfish about how he had acted, he bent down to talk to her.

"Hey, Jilly. Whatcha doing?"

"Making pictures. They're secret presents."

"They're really good."

She grinned up at him.

"I'm really sorry you've had to hang out without us for a while now, but you've been really good about it. Really grown up."

With this, she beamed up at him.

The rest of the afternoon felt like an awful exercise in patience to Jim. He was simply waiting to go back to the farm. It was hard for him to think about anything else.

Finally, it was time.

The sun was going down soon in the deep summer evening, and the family piled into the car. They were going to drive quickly to the farm and sneak in the way that Jim and Jack had been taking. The lateness of the hour hopefully ensured that there weren't too many people out and about. Hopefully.

It was an uneventful journey, with Jilly pointing out everything new that she was seeing. Her excitement was palpable. She had put on her "best" dress, and Jim figured what made it best was that it had the most flowers on it. She had also brought along her fancy pink purse that she liked to take on special occasions. Jim knew she had filled it with the pictures and some snacks.

The road was more busy this evening, so they had to pass by the place once, then return when nobody was around. It would be dark soon, but for now, they were very visible to anyone passing by, so they were careful. Once there, Jilly tumbled out of the Jeep, asking, "Where's Charlie? Charlie!"

"Shhh!" Jim warned. Jilly clamped her mouth shut. "We don't want anyone hearing us. They're going to be a lot further in than this."

Jack nodded at Jim, then turned to lead the way. They walked for quite a while in silence. Jim could tell that Jilly was anxious to speak, but she was good and stayed quiet as she hiked in front of him. Once they were to the spot where they had encountered Scar the night before, Jim and Jack started looking for signs of where to go. It had been a long night and pretty confusing. Jim didn't know that he could find the way.

But that didn't matter. As if waiting for them, Charlie emerged from behind a large oak tree. Jilly couldn't help it and let out a squeal. Her eyes found Karen, who nodded, and Jilly took off running to him. They watched her jump up to the height of Charlie's hips, where he caught her and lifted her high. He hugged her tight and waved to the rest of them. They spent a few minutes as a family, greeting and talking. Charlie listened with a faint smile and looked to be enjoying watching their enthusiasm. It reminded Jim of his pets or small children that don't quite know what's happening but are still enjoying the company and excitement.

When they were ready, Charlie led them the rest of the way to the new family. Jim knew woods and how things could look turned around sometimes, but he was still surprised to see how different everything looked in the failing light. He would have never found this place himself.

They entered the small opening, and Jim could see the thick clump of growth that was their little home. Charlie put out a hand to stop the group at the edge. Nobody was outside of it waiting for them this time. Looking at Jilly, Jim could see her confusion. She was so excited she was practically vibrating with energy, but her face was falling with the absence of the family.

Charlie let out a small grunt and waited. After a few seconds, Jim could hear a small return grunt. As they watched, Scar seemed to materialize in front of them. He was so stealthy in his movements that it was almost like he just suddenly appeared out of nowhere. He moved in front of them, and his eyes locked on Jilly. She was the only one he hadn't yet seen. Despite their size difference and his appearance, Jilly didn't back away or look frightened in any way. She stared right back at him. Finally, she stepped forward, hand outstretched.

"Pleased to meet you. My name's Jilly."

Scar looked at Charlie with an utterly perplexed expression. He looked back down at Jilly, his mouth hanging open. Charlie stepped around to Scar's side and patted him on the shoulder, then scooped Jilly up in his arms. Scar watched with great interest but kept his distance. After a moment, he turned back to his home. He gave a grunt, and the rest of the family emerged.

Jilly gasped. "They're all so cute!"

"I don't know that 'cute' is the right word," Jim muttered under his breath.

Charlie walked forward and set Jilly down. She immediately walked forward to greet them. The young boy bigfoot looked tentatively up at his parents, then stepped forward eagerly. Jilly and the boy studied each other from a few feet away, then moved forward and began looking at each other closely, picking at each other's hair, Jilly's clothes. Jilly giggled the whole time.

Karen began examining the baby. She moved her and the mother a little bit away so that she could listen to the baby with the stethoscope. All appeared to be okay. She gave the baby more antibiotics and a bottle of water. In fact, she gave each of them their own bottles. They all appeared eager for the water. She must have given them some last time, and they wanted more. Jim remembered when he first gave Charlie a bottle of clean water. He had loved it.

Jilly and the boy were now looking at Jilly's pictures, leaning close to the paper to see it better in the dimming light. She had brought some blank paper and crayons to play with, and he was now running multiple crayons over the paper with delight. Jack was with Charlie, who was showing him the inside of the bigfoot home. They were peeking inside, with Scar watching from behind. It was strange watching the two species interact. There was much that was similar and much that was alien to everyone. Jack and Charlie stepped inside the structure, leaving Scar behind. Jim thought he looked somehow more at peace and relaxed. Despite his ferocious appearance, he was a nice being.

As if he sensed Jim's thoughts on him, his face suddenly took on a tense, alert expression. *What?* Scar started moving toward his family. He spoke to them in their strange, guttural language, and they all began running through the woods.

Jim's family was stunned. They didn't know what had happened. Charlie emerged from the home and looked alert, letting them know that something was wrong. He sniffed the air, looked around, then made eye contact with Jim. He pointed firmly back in the direction they had come and shooed them away. He then turned on his heel and disappeared in the direction that Scar's family had gone.

"Let's go," Jack said.

They began a quick walk back, single-file, with Jack leading and Jim bringing up the rear. Jim was straining to hear or see whatever had scared them, but he thought he knew.

Someone was here.

They had almost made it back, when Jack put up a hand. He was staring at something. Karen, who was right behind him, whispered something to him and pointed. They walked over to a tree, and Jim finally saw what they had spotted from in front.

It was a camera.

At first Jim thought that the TV crew had just forgotten this one or overlooked it, but then he realized what was happening. The TV crew hadn't abandoned their investigation. They were doing it secretly. They didn't want Jim and Jack involved.

Jack looked at Jim with a raised eyebrow.

"We can't let them have the footage, Dad. They'll want to know why we were here."

"Let's take care of this."

They grabbed the camera and stopped the recording. Jim deleted it and turned it off. They mounted it back up on the tree, then walked away.

It was a tense walk back to the Jeep, but they made it with no more surprises, though everyone was on the lookout for more cameras and other strange things. When they got in the Jeep and back onto the main road, Jim felt slightly at ease, until he remembered Charlie and the others. He was afraid of whoever had made them hide, and he was afraid of the reason that the TV crew had cut them out of the investigation.

CHAPTER THIRTEEN
Threats

THE NEXT MORNING, they slept a bit later and took a leisurely time getting ready to go, but not before enjoying a big country breakfast at Mel's. The pancakes were bigger than Jim's head, fluffy and sweet. They were the best he had ever had.

Jim was talking about the texture of his delicious pancakes, when an older man approached their table and stood silently. He was staring at them with piercing blue eyes. He had a worn, country appearance, but with his twinkling eyes, he still made a youthful impression on Jim.

"Hi. Can we help you?" Jack asked.

"I know you were asking about, ah, the big fella? So I wanted to let you know that TV crew, they're asking me to help them get this thing they say they saw. They sounded like maybe they meant 'dead or alive' to me."

Jim looked around the table and saw the same shock that he felt.

"Why? Who are you?" Jim sputtered.

The man regarded Jim for a moment. "I'm Dale Walker. See, my daughter says she's seen this thing. In fact, she says it helped her once. Saved her life. I'm not saying it's real, but if it is, whatever it is, it should be left in peace. You seem to have something to do with that crew, but you're different. I thought maybe you could persuade them to move on."

"We certainly agree with you, Mr. Walker," Jack said. "We'll see what we can do."

"What happened to your daughter? What did she see?" Jim asked. He couldn't help but be curious about her experience.

"You can ask her yourself. She's right over there. She would love to tell you about it, I'm sure." He pointed at a slender girl with blonde hair and the same piercing blue eyes. She was at the front corner table, reading a book that was propped up beside her plate of a half-eaten waffle that had been drenched in syrup.

Jim thought she looked cute and nice. Before he had time to think about it, he was on his feet, moving toward her table. He was five feet from her when his brain kicked in, and he realized what he was doing. His mouth went dry and his palms got clammy, but he was going for it. He stopped, and his words came out in a rushed tumble.

"Hi, I'm Jim. Your dad sent me over to ask you about your, um, encounter with, I guess it was a bigfoot?"

She looked at him over the top of her book, then grinned.

"So what do you think?" she asked.

Jim was confused.

"About what?"

"About Bigfoot. You believe he's real?"

Jim smiled. "Sure do."

She sat up straight and put down her book. "Okay, I'll tell you about it. I'm Eva, by the way." She motioned for him to sit, which he did. "So I was out riding my bike one night. Well, it wasn't quite night, but it was late, ya know?"

"Okay."

Her eyes were sparkling.

"We live in a very wooded area, so nobody was around, and I suddenly saw a big, tan cat. I've seen them before in pictures, but never in person. It was a mountain lion. I froze, and it froze in front of me. Then it turned toward me, put its head down, and looked like it was about to pounce. I had no idea what to do, I was so scared."

"Whoa, I would have been, too. Those things are dangerous." Jim was enthralled, mostly because of the story, but also with her.

"I remembered my daddy saying something about trying to look big and not backing down to a big cat, so I guessed staying was better than running. But then it came at me. I turned and tried to run, but I knew it would get me. Then all of a sudden, I heard a screeching sound and growling, so I looked over my shoulder. There was this giant, hairy man-thing, standing there, wrestling with the big cat. It made the cat look like a small house cat."

"Oh wow. That sure is crazy. Was he helping you?"

"I guess so. It seemed like it. But either way, it did save me. It wrestled the cat and threw it, then it looked at me for a few seconds, then it walked into the woods. I was stunned."

"I bet."

"So I hurried home and told my family. We all got in the car and tried to find it, but I haven't seen it since."

She sat back and folded her arms over her chest.

"That's an amazing story," Jim told her, and he meant it.

"I know." She sprang forward again. "It's the best thing that's happened in my life. I wish I could see it again."

"What did it look like, exactly?"

"Had to have been close to maybe ten feet tall? It had dark, shaggy hair all over its body, but it had kind of a smooth part of its face. It had long arms, stood on two legs. It was really cool."

"That sounds just like a bigfoot, you know, how they've been described."

"Yep."

They were quiet for a moment. Jim was feeling more aware of the fact that he was sitting with this pretty girl, having an amazing conversation. He suddenly felt self-conscious.

"So have you seen one?" she asked.

Jim immediately wanted to say that he had, just to have some common ground, but he somehow forced himself to lie.

"Nah, I wish."

He felt bad about lying to her. His cheeks felt hot, and he hoped she wouldn't notice. He suddenly remembered his encounter the other night. Of course he could tell her about that.

"Well, I kinda had an encounter," he sputtered.

Eva perked up.

He sat up straighter. "You know the TV crew here, doing a story about bigfoot?"

"Sure."

"They had me go investigate with them for a couple of days." She raised her eyebrows, impressed. He continued, "The other night, we were chased by something, but we couldn't see it. It was crazy."

"Whoa! That sounds scary." Then she frowned. "And not at all like the bigfoot I saw."

"Maybe he was scared or protecting something."

"Hey, yeah. That could be. Animals do that."

"Hey, Jim," a voice said.

Jim looked up to find the TV crew standing next to the table. Shawna had a strange look on her face, but it wasn't friendly. Pete had a sort of gloating look on his face, but Jim wasn't sure what he would be gloating about, and Larry looked his usual nervous.

"We need to talk," Shawna said.

Jim could tell it wasn't good. It felt wrong.

"Let's go find my family," he said.

"Sure, we should talk to them, too."

As much as he didn't want to, Jim said goodbye to a very confused Eva, then walked through the diner to his family. Karen had seen the exchange and was ushering everyone from the table, toward Jim. They met in the middle.

"They want to talk to us, Mom."

She looked at them, and Jim could see her quickly size up the situation.

"Let's go outside, then." She walked past them, leading the way, without waiting for their agreement. They followed her to the far end of the parking lot, away from anyone who could listen in.

"Okay, what do you need to say?" Karen asked.

Shawna stepped up to Karen. "We know about you and your, hmm, big friend." She was wearing a smug smile.

Nobody said anything.

Shawna continued.

"We had a few cameras up and recorded your whole little family here waltzing up to a freakin' *bigfoot* and acting all friendly with it. It's all recorded."

Karen paused a beat, then, "So what do you want?"

Shawna laughed. "What do we want? Well, we really don't need anything from you. We have the most amazing footage ever recorded, and we can release it immediately. But what we would really like is for you to take us to it. If you do that, we'll hold off on releasing it long enough for you to clear on out of here and go into hiding."

"No deal," Karen said and turned on her heel to walk back to their Jeep. The family followed in stunned silence.

"Wait! Wait. I think we got off on the wrong foot here," Shawna said. Jim couldn't believe she was using so many cliches right now. "I'm sorry I tried the heavy-handed approach, but most people seem to need a firm handling." She took a deep breath and kept going. "We've spent years trying to find proof that they exist, and here it is! It's thrilling. It looked like you have some sort of relationship with this thing. If we could have better proof that it isn't, say, some guy in a costume, it would really go a long way toward getting these guys protected status." Her eyes had a desperate quality.

Jim looked at his mom. She looked to have softened a bit but not much. Shawna really messed up by taking the approach she had initially.

Jack stepped forward. "We understand what you mean, but we can't do that. If you saw what you say you saw, then you know what he means to us. We can't let anything happen to him. There's a situation here that you don't understand."

"Then help us understand."

"Just please don't release that footage."

"Look, I have to. People have to know."

"Please leave it alone."

"We'll have to agree to disagree. I hope you come to your senses. People should know. It will help the species."

"We will have to disagree." Jack looked at his family. "Let's go."

They piled into the car as quickly as they could. Jim was really worried. He had hoped that nobody would ever find out about Charlie again, but this was out of their control.

"What do we do?" Jim asked. "They're going to go after him. They need more than just a video. People will think it's a guy in a costume."

"I know. We need to get him out of here and warn the others." He paused for a moment. "At least they want to protect the species."

Karen spoke up. "I understand that, and it's good, but I don't think our family needs to worry about that. Charlie's had a rough time and doesn't need any more problems. We promised to take care of him, and we can't take on the whole species, you know, protecting them."

Jim was conflicted. He definitely wanted to protect Charlie, but meeting Scar and his family made him realize that there really are more out there who deserve good lives, too. He wanted to protect them, just like Charlie. In reality, he knew he couldn't do that, but maybe they should try to talk to Shawna. She could help by leaving them alone.

"Do you think that one day people need to know about them? For the sake of the species?" Jack asked her.

Karen stared out the window for a moment. Nobody said anything. Jim could see the point, but he instinctively felt like nobody should know. He wondered if that was warranted, if he was selling humans too short.

No. Despite the many people who believed in bigfoot, there were more who did not. This would be a shock to everyone, especially them. There would be scientists hoping to study them, hunters wanting a trophy, even if they were a protected species. Since when has that stopped people? There would be issues with people deciding how to live with them, people wanting to see them in zoos or in their natural habitats. It would be too much. Right now, they're doing well on their own. Or so he hoped. But they weren't the focus of much attention. If they were proven to exist, they would become the focus. He didn't want to find out how everyone in the world viewed them and wanted to treat them.

He just couldn't trust people right now. Not after the way the Whittles had acted a year ago and seeing how desperate Shawna looked now.

When they arrived back at their RV, they took a moment to recover. Everyone sat quietly, thinking. Finally, Jack said, "We need to go get Charlie. Now. But we need to be careful. Let's get out of here."

"But, Dad, we can't just leave the others. The baby needs help, and the others could get captured or something. They're not safe," Jim argued.

"The baby does need to keep taking its antibiotics. Can't just stop in the middle," Karen pointed out.

Jack pursed his lips. Jim knew it would be easiest just to get Charlie and disappear, but they couldn't do that. It would be hard to tell the mother bigfoot how to give antibiotics. That was just beyond their capabilities, most likely.

"Let's go see Charlie, at least. We need to get him back here with us, so we can watch over him."

CHAPTER FOURTEEN
Visit

THEY MADE THE trip to the farm in record time. Most people from the town were working, so the roads weren't too busy. They pulled in and walked a different route, away from the farm house, and came in from the opposite side, near the spot that they had met Charlie. It took a good ten minutes of sitting and waiting for Charlie before they heard the familiar purr of his call.

Everyone was tense. Nobody spoke. And when they finally did, it was in whispers. Jack had brought binoculars and had been scouting the area for cameras, but they saw nothing. When Charlie finally greeted them, they all felt better knowing he was okay. He still seemed very happy and in a bit of a daze.

Jim knew it was weird and exciting for him to be with his own kind, but he also thought he saw a wariness and desire to be back with his family. Maybe he was only hoping and projecting his own thoughts on him. He certainly hoped Charlie wanted to continue to live with them.

"Hey, Charlie. How are you?" he asked his friend.

Charlie responded with a hug and a smile. He patted Jim's head and looked around at the family. Then he turned and led them back to the others. It was a longer walk, and they found the others in another, thicker section of woods.

They had moved.

The mother bigfoot appeared from behind a tree with Scar, holding her baby. Her eyes immediately found Karen, and she stepped forward eagerly. Karen checked the baby and announced that her breathing sounded better, and she appeared to be feeling better. She gave the baby more medicine, and the mother looked soothed as she gently rocked her baby and made soft cooing sounds to it. Jim was struck by how human this gesture was, coming from something like her.

Jim's attention was drawn to Jack, who was trying to impart to Charlie the danger they were in. He was pointing in the direction of the farm and talking about the people they had been with. Charlie's eyes were narrowed, and his mouth was slightly open as he concentrated on Jack's words and movements. He was obviously trying very hard to understand what Jack was saying. By carefully using body language, tone, and simple words, Jack was finally able to convey their message: Charlie needed to come with them, the others needed to hunker down there, away from the prying eyes of the TV crew. They would figure things out later.

Jim looked to Jilly, who had immediately found her new friend, the young boy. They had engaged in a drawing session using Jilly's marker set. Jilly was showing him her finished pictures in her Disney coloring book and how to stay in the lines. The boy gasped in delight at the colorful images of cartoon characters engaged in fun activities. Jim wanted to take pictures of the two of them, but he didn't. They were quite a pair, sitting on the bare ground of the forest, coloring like human children. Jilly's long sheet of copper hair covered her back, making her look like a cute creature from behind.

Jim smiled. He felt a presence behind him and turned to find Charlie standing there, looking at the same scene Jim had been admiring. His smile showed Jim he appreciated the same qualities that Jim did.

Looking at Charlie, he realized how much he had been missing him. This was something he had been wanting to do for him, but now that Charlie had found others, he was afraid that he would leave them. They had been so busy that Jim hadn't had enough time to really think about it. But now, looking at him, he was filled with sadness and anxiety.

"Charlie, I've missed you."

Charlie's eyes flicked down to Jim. He looked perplexed for a moment, then he seemed to understand Jim's worry and sadness. He reached out and pulled Jim to him in a rough embrace that Jim likened to two best friends who didn't want to get too gooey with their emotions. It was still funny to have thoughts like that—thoughts that compared Charlie to humans. There was such a human-like quality, yet he obviously wasn't human.

What was he?

"Jim, we should leave Charlie here again. It could be too dangerous to have him come out of hiding and be among the little town. He's safe here for now," Jack said. He was standing with Karen and had obviously been talking with her about the situation.

"I agree with your dad. He would have to make it out of the woods, the ride in the car, from the car to the RV …"

They were right. The bigfoot had hidden well enough so far, and now they knew they were in danger, so they would be even more careful. At least Jim hoped they would.

The rest of the visit was tense for Jim. He kept expecting someone to pop out at them. And knowing that they would be leaving Charlie again was gnawing at him. He tried to put those thoughts out of his mind, but it was no use.

Charlie seemed to sense his uneasiness and tried his best to comfort Jim. He stayed by his side and kept patting his shoulder and giving him reassuring looks. It made Jim feel a bit better.

Finally, it was time to go. The family said their goodbyes to their hairy friends and made Charlie stay there while they hiked out. He didn't need to leave the safety of their new hiding place to walk them out—they could make it on their own. The ride back to the RV was quiet. Each was, again, lost in their own thoughts.

Jack spoke first.

"Let's just keep doing what we've been doing and try our best to avoid the TV crew. It's not the best plan, but it's really the only one. There isn't much we can do."

"Yeah, we're stuck," Karen said.

CHAPTER FIFTEEN
Town Buzz

THEY GOT READY for a late dinner and headed out to the diner. It was crowded again. Most of the town that wasn't doing any cooking at home was sitting at tables all over Mel's. Many were up and about, visiting with friends. When Jim and his family entered, a quiet settled over the entire place. It took several seconds as word quietly spread, so Jim didn't notice it at first. But when he did, it was eerie. He looked up and found most eyes upon their family.

"Uh … what's going on?" Jim said out of the corner of his mouth.

"I don't know, but does anyone else feel like leaving?" Jack asked.

Jim was about to agree, when he saw Eva slicing through the crowd toward them. He took an involuntary step forward to greet her. When she finally made it through, she smiled and said, "Hey."

"Hey. What's going on?" Jim looked warily at the rest of the diner.

"Oh, that. Weirded you out, huh? Word's spread that you guys are involved with the bigfoot people. Everyone wants to know what's going on."

"Didn't you already know? Seems like a small town would already know what they're up to."

"Nah, somebody said they're out at the Hoke place, but Mr. Hoke hasn't been seen around town in years. He's kinda been hiding out since his wife died."

"The guy at the store seemed to know about it."

"Sure, he knows they're hanging out there, but not what's going on. Like, details." She looked past Jim, to his family. "Hi, I'm Eva."

Karen and Jack both smiled at her.

"Hi, Eva. I'm Karen, and this is my husband Jack, and our daughter Jilly."

"Jilly? I like that name."

"I like you; you're pretty and smiley," Jilly said with a blush. Eva had already won Jilly over. Despite her easy acceptance of the bigfoot and Eva, Jilly was a picky person. People had to prove themselves to her.

"Don't mind them," she said, glancing over her shoulder. "They're just curious about what that TV crew's been doing at the Hoke place."

"I'm sure they are," Jack said. "We were curious, too. Really, though, they haven't seen or heard much during their investigations."

"They came to interview some people a couple of days ago, but most didn't want to talk to them. We're all curious about what they're doing as far as this so-called 'investigation' and what they've seen. I told them about your run-in with whatever it was while you were investigating with them." Looking at Jim's parents, she explained, "Jim said there was something that chased him and them the other night. Everyone wants to know about that and whatever else you've been up to."

Jim felt himself go red. His parents looked at him in surprise. They weren't supposed to be adding to any curiosity about a bigfoot in the area; they weren't supposed to be increasing any interest and possibly any more bigfoot hunters. Jack gave him a look like he knew exactly why he had done it, but he wasn't happy about it.

Mel's hubbub had slowly picked back up, but there were still plenty of people sneaking looks in their direction.

"There they are!"

The family looked up to see Eva's dad moving through the crowd to meet them. His eyes were shining with excitement, his face friendly.

"How are you this evening? Don't let the attention bother you. You're sorta like celebrities right now. Come, we have a table for you. Join us!" He turned, and they all shrugged and began to follow him.

Mr. Walker had a large table in the far corner of the diner. A woman who looked a lot like Eva was sitting next to an empty chair and another couple who reminded Jim of parents from one of those old TV shows with the perfect family was waiting with her. The woman had an old-fashioned dress and a string of pearls, and the man was wearing a suit. They looked slightly out of place here. The group was sitting at one of the tables for a larger party, so Jim and his family would fit easily. Apparently nobody worried too much about a large party showing up—they all knew each other and who might be eating there.

Mr. Walker said, "Sit, sit. Let me introduce you to the mayor of our little town, Phil Daniels, and his wife Betty. They're originally from the Dallas area, but they joined us a couple decades ago, just about."

Mr. Daniels stood and shook hands all around. "How do you do? I've heard a lot about you." Mrs. Daniels smiled demurely and nodded to each family member.

"Now let me introduce you to my wife, Gracie" They all said hello politely.

Introductions over, the group got down to business. Mr. Daniels began, "Now Jack, can I call you 'Jack'?" He didn't wait for an answer. "Well, Jack, I hear your family got roped into goin' on some sort of investigations with those TV folks. What was goin' on there?" He started to remind Jim of the mayor from that movie *Jaws*. Jim pictured him in a jacket covered with little anchors and nearly laughed.

"Oh that." Jack laughed. "Well, my son here, he's interested in that sort of thing and—"

"Ah, what sort of thing? Just so we're all clear here," Mr. Daniels said.

"Bigfoot," Jack said strongly. The group from Bisby gave each other knowing glances and fidgeted uncomfortably.

All except Mr. Walker.

Jack continued, "So he was familiar with the TV crew, he approached them and asked what they were doing, and they asked him to come along. They thought it would be a nice angle to have a young, interested guy come along for an investigation."

"And?"

"And what?"

Mr. Daniels gave a little laugh. "Well, we heard that your son encountered somethin' with them." The man was leaning forward, practically hovering in the air in front of Jack.

"That's true," Jack said slowly, hesitantly. "I'm not sure how much we can say since this is supposed to be part of their show."

"I understand, I understand," Mr. Daniels said as his face fell. He looked around the room for a moment, thinking. "But it's just between us, here at the table. I am the mayor and should know if there's anything that the good people of this town should be worried about. Besides, word is already spreadin' since your boy told Eva. And word is good! It'll only fuel the fire of curiosity. People will watch the show. Good for the TV people, good for the town of Bisby." He winked at that. "But, while word is good, the word needs to say the right thing, you know." He looked pointedly at Jack.

"What I can say is that there's nothing to worry about." Mr. Daniels opened his mouth to speak, but Jack hurried on. "There was something that didn't want us to be near it, but that's true of most animals out here, right? We don't know what it was, but that's not to say that it was a bigfoot or anything dangerous. I certainly am not worried." He emphasized these last words.

"Great, great." Mr. Daniels clapped his hands together. "This is great news. I know that there's some talk around here about certain folks seein' somethin', uh, odd around here. But I know there are many people who would be truly frightened to know somethin' like that was hidin' out here in our quiet town. I also know plenty of hunters who could get out of control if they were to start lookin' for this thing. And I know this town doesn't want an influx of out-of-towners comin' here, tramplin' all over private property with guns or cameras or whatever. I know they'd be spendin' money …" he said with a hungry glint in his eye, but he carried on, "but I don't think many here would take too kindly to somethin' like that, and I could see somethin' like this gettin' out of hand. So this is great news!"

"Glad to make you feel better," Jack said with a tight smile.

"Maybe I can talk to the crew about includin' some of our history and tourist sights …" he said, almost to himself. Obviously, his mind was already working on planning a marketing strategy.

Jim didn't like this. The mayor certainly didn't want a bigfoot running around here. Or at least he wanted people to hear about Bisby but not to go crazy with the bigfoot thing. Jim would have thought that the man would welcome visitors of any kind and their money, but he could also see how something like this could get out of hand.

"Let's eat!" Mr. Daniels exclaimed. They spent the rest of the evening hearing about the history of the town, its most prominent or interesting residents, and any little stories the group felt would interest Jim's family. Jim was actually surprised at how entertaining such a small town could be.

As they ate, people kept coming up to the table to greet the mayor and Mr. Walker. They all seemed to respect these men. And each of the visitors had to mention their take on bigfoot and the TV crew. Unfortunately, the majority wanted no real part in the matter and were worried that any type of publicity would bring annoyances to the town. Jim could see these particular people were conflicted. Each wanted more visitors, but they were private people with large pieces of land, mostly with cattle or other livestock or crops. These things provided their livelihoods, and they couldn't have people accidentally trespassing on their land. Mr. Daniels kept reassuring them, but also slyly encouraging the idea of more tourists to the area. Jim was impressed with his skills.

Practically the only people who didn't come up to their table were two guys. They were two of the group of three guys who had been there the first night. Jim realized that the two looked eerily similar. Same narrow bodies, same eyes. One was older and more withered than the other, but they both looked like they had worked outside all their lives and could take care of themselves. They must be brothers. The third guy wasn't there, and Jim remembered him looking very little like these two. They were tucked into the corner, backs to the walls, and watching the proceedings. Their crossed arms and fierce faces told Jim that they didn't approve of what was happening. He just wasn't sure what their deal was, exactly.

"Mr. Walker, who are those guys?" Jim asked.

Mr. Walker looked at Jim, then where he was pointing. He almost grimaced when his eyes found the table, and he looked back at Jim and exhaled slowly. "Those guys are the Mortons. They own the land behind Hoke's place. They're one of the oldest families in town, and they don't like all this new stuff happening. Back in the day, way back, they were always fighting with the Hokes about their property line. Since Hoke's been gone, they've been trying to get his land. They're greedy and mean. They, in particular, have been very interested in the TV crew and what they're doing. I can't decide if they hate it, or if they want a cut of whatever they can get out of it, but they're watching everything closely."

Mr. Walker turned back to the table as the mayor let out a loud guffaw, and the conversation moved to stories about one of their more colorful residents in history, a man named Cross-eyed Hank. People kept coming up to their table and expressing the same feelings as the previous load of people. Especially a little, old woman named Mrs. Templeton. She looked so frail that a good gust of wind could take her away, but she was fierce and strong. She was sure to let her feelings known—she did not want anyone meddling in her town.

Jim was happy that these people weren't anxious to look for Charlie or Scar and his family. He figured they represented a good part of the town, so hopefully the bigfoot family was safe.

The TV crew were the only ones threatening them now.

CHAPTER SIXTEEN
About-face

THE NEXT MORNING, Jim and his family made another quick trip out to see Charlie. The whole family was going now that the TV crew was out of the picture. As they walked through the woods, Jim felt better about things. They hadn't heard from Shawna and her crew in a couple of days, and he had been checking their website multiple times a day for the video of them visiting Charlie.

Nothing yet.

The birds were out in full force, chirping and flitting around above their heads. A fat rabbit popped out in front of them, scaring everyone until they realized it was only a rabbit, then they shared a quiet laugh. Jilly took things a bit too far and began her squeaky laugh while trying her best to stifle it. She only got squeaky when she got really tickled about something. They all had to shush her and wait out her laughing fit. When she was quiet, they carried on with their relaxing hike.

Suddenly, Jim heard a quiet shuffle and looked to the right. Charlie was standing partially obscured behind a tree, watching them. He raised a hand in greeting, a smile on his face. As they greeted him, Jim noticed that his naturally deep-set eyes looked more hooded and wary.

He was tired.

"How are you doing, Charlie?" Jim asked him quietly.

He looked at Jim and sighed. Reading the concern on Jim's face and in his voice, he gave Jim a small smile and a pat on the head. He then turned and led the group to the hidden family. They were still in their new hiding place and still cautious.

That was good.

The secret family was visibly happy to see the Thomas family. Their wariness of them seemed less, and they had excitement and eagerness in their eyes. This time, the mother handed her baby over to Karen, who had never held such a baby in her arms. Karen sat down with the mother and cooed at the baby and bounced it gently on a knee. She looked up at Jack and Jim with gleaming eyes, apparently overcome with the joy of the moment.

Charlie tapped Jim on the shoulder. He lifted his own shoulder and shrugged it in the direction of the area where the bigfoot family had been sleeping. Jim followed him over there. They bent down and Charlie pointed at a group of objects in the brush. They were rocks. But not just rocks—they were tools. A couple of them appeared to be worn into sharp knife-like objects. Another was worn into a very crude type of spoon. The others were similar— they had tools. Jim wasn't surprised. Charlie had always been very smart—smart enough to understand their language somewhat, smart enough to use a water bottle. This was proof that Charlie's intelligence wasn't just unique to him.

"Dad, you have to look at these." He got up and left the confines of the bushes to let his dad in his place. He glanced at Jilly, who was quietly singing a song for the little boy. He was sitting cross-legged in front of Jilly, mouth hanging open, listening to her tune. She wasn't the best singer, but it was still enjoyable. Jim thought it was a theme song to one of the Disney cartoons Jilly loved so much.

He sat down by the pair, since he hadn't spent much time with the boy. Jim realized he was so young. His eyes were bright, and his hair was soft and lighter in color than either Scar or his mother's. He looked at Jim with wide, open eyes. Jim felt like he could see his personality. He could feel the wonder in him, the curiosity. Jim smiled at him and said, "Hi. Are you enjoying the song?"

"Course he is! Everyone loves this song," Jilly said. "It's fun."

Jim laughed. As he did, the boy leaned forward. It reminded Jim of his dog when Jim made a funny sound or whistled at him. His ears would perk up, and he would cock his head to one side while he listened hard. The boy didn't do this, but his interest in the funny sound was clear.

He was suddenly aware of Charlie, who had quietly walked closer to watch them all interact. Glancing up, Jim saw Charlie's eyes shone with happiness.

Scar made a sharp grunting noise that snapped everyone's attention to him. His eyes were wide, mouth open; he was sniffing deeply while rocking his weight from side to side. He looked alarmed. Turning quickly, he grabbed his son and made an urgent noise to his mate, who snatched the baby from Karen. They all swiftly moved away from Jim's family, slipping into the woods, leaving Jim puzzled and startled. He started to look at Jack for answers but saw that he and the rest of his family were just as confused and tense as he was.

A crack broke the buzzing atmosphere. Jim had trouble comprehending what had happened. At first he thought that a tree branch had broken, but Scar's reaction told him that it had been a gunshot.

Someone had shot at them. But who? Why?

He ducked down and moved quickly to Jilly and Karen, who seemed frozen in place. Karen was the first of the two to respond by ducking and moving to Jilly, simultaneously. Jim reached Jilly at the same time, and they pulled her down beside them. Jack came out of the little sleeping spot at a crouch and moved to join his family, with Charlie right on his heels. They all looked around, trying to locate the source of danger, but whoever it was, they were well hidden.

Jim was getting tired of being shot at. This wasn't the first time he had been shot at since he met Charlie, but he was going to make sure it was the last. Charlie started to raise up and another shot rang out. Luckily this person was a bad shot—Jim heard it hit the trees far above and to the right of any of them.

Still, they were pinned.

A crashing noise was becoming louder now. Jim was confused until Jack said, "They're coming! We need to get out of here." He turned to Charlie and said, "Go, get yourself out of here." But Charlie wasn't leaving his family in danger. He looked at Jack with a hard-set jaw and stony eyes. He grunted and looked in the direction of the threat, then puffed out his chest. Jim realized how scary he could be when defending his family. Whoever this was, they had no idea what they were dealing with.

The family crawled together and got behind a couple of large trees. The sounds were coming closer, and Jim could hear a deep, rumbling growl resonating from Charlie's barrel of a chest.

It was the most intimidating thing Jim had ever heard.

Everyone's attention was on the approaching noise, when Jim heard a faint sound behind them. Charlie heard it too, and they both turned quickly. Something was moving behind a tree thirty feet from them.

The shooting threat approaching them was still growing near, but whoever they were, for there was more than one person, they were moving more carefully now. However, Jim was now focused on the noise behind them. A light object peeked at them from behind a tree, and Jim was surprised to see a face.

It was Shawna!

She spotted them and reached out a hand, waving them over.

Jim was dumbfounded. He had pretty much assumed that she and her crew were involved in this, but here she was, waving them over. Was it a trick? Scare them into a trap? He saw her roll her eyes, and she disappeared behind the tree again. She reappeared with binoculars. He watched her scan the area behind them, then she moved out from behind the tree in a crouch. She practically duck-walked to them in seconds.

"Hey, Jim. You guys gotta come with me. These guys want this thing dead." As she mentioned Charlie, she looked at him. The sight of him this close for the first time appeared to take her breath away, because she gasped and stared. Charlie stared back, then looked at Jim, who nodded at him to tell him she was okay.

At least he hoped.

She shook her head, blinked, and appeared to rejoin them in the present. "They're some farmers who couldn't resist the chance to bag a bigfoot. Pete's getting everything packed, and the van's ready to go. I can get you all out of here. Larry's helping."

Jack narrowed his eyes with skepticism. "Thanks, but we have our Jeep ready to go, and we can find our way out."

"Sure, but you need help distracting these bozos."

"That we'll take you up on," Jack said.

"Okay, head back that way," she said, nodding behind her.

Jim was worried about her. "Be careful. This could be dangerous."

She smiled at him. "Not to worry. I've been in worse situations."

Jim doubted it, but he wasn't about to argue.

Shawna let out a yell that made everyone jump, "Hey! You jerks! You're going to hit me!"

Jack waved his family and Charlie away, while Shawna stepped out from behind the trees they had been hiding behind, arms waving.

Jim could hear her yelling at the hunters. Suddenly, a deep growling mixed with whoops sounded far to their right, closer to where the family had lived before. Jim was momentarily confused, then he heard Shawna yell, "There it is! Let's go find it." She was leading them away. Larry must have been playing a recording of a bigfoot to draw them away. Jim hoped he didn't get shot by accident, or even shot at. The guy was nervous enough as it was.

They moved at a quick pace through the woods. It took them a while to get to their Jeep, but they arrived without any problems. The problem now was fitting them all inside. Charlie was too big; he took up too much room. Jim and Jilly had to sit in the rear cargo space for the short ride back to the RV park.

They entered the RV quickly and stealthily got Charlie inside, but the day was late enough that most of the RV park inhabitants were off exploring the area or inside because of the midday heat. Without much talk, everyone began packing up to leave as quickly as possible. They all had the same idea: to get out of there. The only regrets were not getting the bigfoot family safely hidden, and the baby wouldn't be able to finish its course of antibiotics. But Jim's family had to put their own safety first.

Jim and Jack were outside, taking down the tent and beginning to unhook the RV, when they heard the sound of a vehicle. Walking around to the front, they saw the TV crew's van slowly approaching. The sight made Jim's stomach tighten. Jim thought it looked like a giant, black beetle moving along a dirt path. There was nothing to do but wait to see what they wanted.

The van pulled up and Shawna was out first, followed by Pete and a very twitchy Larry. Looking closely, Jim noticed there was something else to Larry now, but he couldn't quite figure it out. He was still twitching and jerking his head to look all around himself, but he also seemed to be holding his head higher, and his eyes were more focused. He almost looked proud and excited.

Shawna stopped in front of them. "Everyone okay?"

"We are. You guys get out okay?" Jack asked.

The corner of Shawna's mouth pulled into a slight, lopsided grin. "We were fine. Larry had rigged up a recording to play from his phone. It was pretty genius of him. He wasn't too close when it played. You should have seen them! They went running, all wild-eyed. They thought they saw a bigfoot at every turn. Finally convinced them to leave or there would be hell to pay, *since they almost shot me*. Wink, wink."

Jim was impressed, but he was still unclear about something. "Who were they? What were they doing there in the first place?"

Shawna's smile faltered. She looked at Pete and Larry, who wouldn't make eye contact now and were shifting uncomfortably.

"Uh, they were some Morton family? Well, they had contacted us about what we were doing and what we had seen. We had interviewed them before. Interviewed most of the town, right?" She feebly turned to Pete and Larry for some sort or backup. Jim noticed the guys still wouldn't make eye contact and apparently had lost their voices. "So they asked us about finding proof and helping us. We said no at first, but they said they knew how to track animals, and they said they were bringing their guns just for protection. And after what happened before, we thought it wasn't a bad idea. But …"

Jim and Jack just stood there, not saying a word. They weren't going to make the situation more comfortable for her.

"We kinda also thought maybe shooting it was a good idea just to prove it existed. You know, sacrifice one to save the rest? Anyway, it was a bad idea, and when we sneaked up on you guys, we quickly saw what they really wanted to do. Those woods were so thick that all we could see was the top of his shoulders up," she said, looking around for Charlie. "We really had no idea you guys were there. I know they didn't either. Not that it makes things okay, I know."

"Didn't they see us when they got closer?" Jack asked incredulously.

"Oh yeah. They freaked out. You people might want to lay low for a while. Or get out of here."

"We're heading out as soon as we can."

"Okay," she said quietly. "But we're sorry we brought this trouble on you guys. We want to help now."

"Why?" Jim asked. "Why do you want to help now? After all this time, hunting them and bringing those guys in to actually kill one, why would you want to help us or a bigfoot now?"

She stared hard at him and took a deep breath. "We saw how out of control things can get, and so quickly. These guys seemed okay one second and the next second, boom, their eyes are wild, and they're shooting like crazy, not even caring if they hit a person. They didn't care about our safety for sure, and they obviously didn't put yours first. Then we saw your friend and how you were interacting with him again … that was amazing. We sort of never really thought of a bigfoot being so … human? I guess that's close. It was just a sudden feeling that we needed to protect him. And you. Afterward, we talked about it. On the way out of the woods and over here. We were thinking about all the stuff your friend would have to go through if they caught him alive somehow. We also thought it would be a terrible thing for him to die if there are others of him out there. They should be a protected species."

Shawna was quiet for a moment, and Jim could see her thinking. She looked to be trying to decide something. Her mouth was twitching; she licked her lips. Pete and Larry were staring hard and kept stealing glances at Shawna. They were waiting for something.

"So, uh, are there two?"

"Two what?" Jim asked, playing stupid.

Shawna looked at him, but there was no cynicism, no smugness, no anger, just anxious curiosity. "Two bigfoot," she said quietly. "Pete swears the one we saw the other night was darker, bigger … just different."

Jim shared a look with Jack. What do they do? The crew already knows they exist. They already saw Charlie. Jim felt that Jack was thinking the same things. They shared an almost mental conversation, then Jack nodded, and Jim returned the nod.

She filled the silence. "We thought we saw another one before the shooting, too."

They must have seen the two tallest ones over the bigfoot home.

Jack cleared his throat. "Actually, there are a lot more than that, I suspect."

"But right here?" Jim continued, "There are five total. That we know about."

Shawna's mouth dropped open. Pete and Larry broke into grins.

So Larry can grin.

"You've got to be kidding me," Shawna said. "What's the deal? Who are you people? You have to tell us."

Jim felt like they had helped them save themselves and Charlie. He liked what Shawna had said, but he still wasn't sure.

"Look, thanks for helping us out. Really. But we just don't want to get in the middle of things," Jack said. "We're leaving, and we'd appreciate you not naming us or publishing anything about us."

Shawna almost started answering before Jack had finished. "I'm so sorry—we—all of us—are so sorry. We talked about it. We can see why you would want to keep things quiet and that we were wrong."

They stood facing each other, the two groups.

Finally, Jack spoke. "Come inside. It'll be a tight squeeze."

CHAPTER SEVENTEEN
Allies

JIM TURNED TO hurry into the RV. He went up the steps and pulled open the door. "Guys! Incoming. Charlie, get in the bedroom."

Charlie's head snapped up. He looked confused, but he obviously sensed the urgency in Jim's voice and recognized the word "bedroom." He stood from the couch and lumbered, hunched over, into the bedroom and sat down just as the door opened.

"Go on inside," he heard Jack say.

Shawna was first. She looked around as she entered the RV. "Nice place. It's roomy and cozy."

"We love it," Karen said from the dinette. "Come in and have a seat."

"Thanks, ma'am," Pete said. He was staring at the table that Karen had set up with sandwich ingredients and chips and fruit. He licked his lips.

Jilly was sitting at the table, eating a cheese sandwich and strawberries. "Who are you? Are you the TV people?" she asked.

"Hi there," Shawna said with a smile. "Yes, we're the TV people. But we're not doing that anymore."

Jim wondered what that meant, but he kept quiet. They would get to it.

Shawna sat on the couch closest to the dinette, Larry plopped down the other end, and Pete took the middle. They were sitting there like small children—backs straight, eyes wide. It looked slightly funny to Jim. They looked anxious and uncomfortable.

"So you want to know who we are. This won't be published anywhere? Won't be put on your blog or website or anything?" Jack asked.

"I promise you that nothing we say here will ever leave this room, or RV. We're out of this business." Larry and Pete nodded vigorously. Pete was more careful about his nodding because his face looked like it felt terrible. It was bruised and swollen from his fall a couple of nights ago.

Jack blew out a breath. "Okay. So we live a few hours from here, but in Texas. Last year, we met someone who changed our lives and the way we look at the world. Jim did, actually. He saved Jim, and they became friends."

"He saved me, too!" Jilly yelled.

"He did?" Shawna asked, her voice getting higher to talk to little Jilly. "What did he save you from?"

"A mommy pig tried to hurt me, because she was protecting her baby. But Charlie came and saved me. Jimmy tried to save me, too, but Charlie's stronger." She finished with a proud smile and her hazel eyes shining.

"Whoa, that's scary," Pete said, shaking his head.

"That is scary. I'm glad you're okay," Shawna added.

Larry cleared his throat, his mouth popped open, then closed. Finally he said, "Uh, 'Charlie'?"

Shawna nodded, her hair bouncing on her shoulders. "Yes, you said that name. Is that his name?"

"Yeah," Jim confirmed. "He's my best friend." He felt his throat tighten and didn't try to say anything else.

Jim felt the RV rock and heard a soft noise behind him. He turned to find the partition opening, and Charlie poked his head out. There were gasps from the couch, then Charlie moved his large body all the way out, completely filling up the open space between the bathroom door and the shower.

"Oh my God."

"This can't be real."

Jim heard Pete and Larry grappling with the sight from behind him and smiled while watching Charlie. Charlie looked interested and patient. It was like he was studying the new people and allowing them time to come to terms with what they were seeing before he did anything else. It was amazing to see him grow and adapt.

"Can I see him up close?" Shawna's voice came from right behind Jim. He turned to look at her. She was staring up at Charlie, with her mouth open. Her eyes were big and unblinking. It was almost as if she felt that if she did blink, he would disappear.

"Sure. Charlie, this is Shawna. Shawna, Charlie." Jim squeezed by her and let her stand before Charlie.

"Dude, I wish I could record this," Pete said.

"But you can't," Jack said with finality.

"I know, I know. Just sayin'."

"Pete, please. I'm meeting the most amazing creature ever, and I don't want it tainted," Shawna said, not taking her eyes off Charlie. "Hello, Charlie. Thrilled to meet you. For real." She stuck out her hand and laughed nervously, then started to drop it, like she felt silly for having done that automatically.

But Charlie reached out and grabbed her hand. He had learned to shake a while ago, despite not meeting anyone else. Jilly had taught him.

The three newcomers erupted in cheers and laughter, while the Thomas family laughed at their excitement.

"Oh man! This is the most amazing thing I've ever seen. Dude, Larry, are you seeing this?" Pete slapped Larry's back a bit too hard, but Larry barely seemed to notice.

"Incredible," Larry squeaked. He was actually smiling.

Shawna looked at Jim, and he was taken by how radiant she looked. Her auburn hair was framing her glowing face, and her eyes were shining and piercing. Her look was that of pure joy. Jim was reminded of the way Jilly looks on Christmas morning.

"So what can he do?"

Jim looked at Karen, who scrunched her face in a "what?" expression. "Uh, what do you mean?" he asked.

"I mean, I know he's not, like, a dog or anything, but what's he capable of? Can he speak? Does he understand us? Where did he come from? Does he have a family? What is he? Is—"

"You ask a lot of questions," Jilly interrupted.

Shawna stopped, frozen. Then she laughed. "It's just so incredible! How can I not ask questions? I need answers."

"Well," Jim was trying to think back to when he had first met Charlie. What had surprised him? "He came from somewhere else, and we gather a fire sent him away from his home, where he did have a family. He's a young bigfoot. He understands a lot, like an insane amount of words and things we do. He can't really speak like us. He can sort of say little things, but it's kind of like how a parrot can mimic some things, only I think he understands more. I've done some research on why apes can't speak, and it has something to do with how their throats are different. I guess that's the deal with him. I don't know."

"Wow. Okay, so you're saying you all think he's like an ape?"

Jim looked at his parents. Everyone was quiet for a moment. It was a question they had been grappling with.

"We're not sure," Karen answered. "He's certainly not a gorilla, although his size is more along those lines. It's almost like he's in between us and them, but closer to which, we don't know. That would be something for experts to determine."

"Sure. I see what you're saying."

Pete spoke up from the couch. "Those experts would love to get their hands on him. Ohhh boy. There would be tons of them, lining up, ready to poke at him, do whatever." He finished by shaking his head.

"Yeah, think about it, guys," Larry leaned forward. Everyone turned to him, and when they did, he started to sink back into the couch, but he stopped and suddenly sat up straight. He was really changing. "Right now, he has a nice home, it looks like. He has people who care about him, and he's safe. Well, safe enough. If anyone knows about him, he, at the very least, would be considered an endangered species. He would be taken away from you, most likely. I'm ashamed to say I've never really thought about what would happen if one was found, but now ..." It looked like his courage was used up, and he slowly started to slink back into the couch behind Pete.

Everyone was silent for a moment, partly from the shock of so many consecutive words coming from Larry, and partly because they were digesting what he had said. Larry had succinctly put into words the thoughts and feelings that Jim had been experiencing.

"He's right, man," Pete said. Everyone murmured their agreement.

As they talked, Charlie picked up his plate of fruit and started eating. His eyes were roving over the group, and he looked at peace in this moment.

"You should leave," Shawna said. Her eyes were fierce again. Determined. "Go home and stay quiet. We'll try to hedge things here."

"We are. We—" Jack was cut off.

"We can't leave," Karen said. "The baby needs its medication. The others need our help. We stirred this up, and now we're just going to leave them?"

Jim was sort of surprised but not really. Surprised because his parents always put family first, and right now, their family was having trouble. He wasn't surprised, on the other hand, because his parents were also ones to do the right thing. His mom was right. They couldn't leave now.

"But, Mom, how do we go about this with people getting all stirred up? These guys saw us and have probably already told over half the town," Jim pointed out.

"I don't know, honey, but we'll figure something out. We always do."

"And you're not alone now. We'll help," Shawna said.

CHAPTER EIGHTEEN
Hiding Out

THE FIRST THING they decided to do was to have the TV crew go to Mel's and find out what was being said around the town. Jim's family was going to leave the RV park, and Pete would let them onto the Hoke property. Behind the house, a little ways away, there was a large barn where they could park the RV for a short time, while looking like they had left town. It felt like too simple of a plan, but it was the best they could do. Jim reminded himself that sometimes the simplest plans are the best and least expected.

Jim helped Jack pack everything up. They went to the office and checked out, telling the manager that they were heading home. The manager acted like nothing had happened, so they figured word hadn't spread that quickly. They made a show of leaving and drove out onto the main road heading out of town.

Out of town, or at least one way out of town, would take them past Hoke Farm. They went beyond the farm and were relieved to see that not too many people were on the road right now. It was still early in the day, so most people were at work. One truck went by. It was full of teenagers listening to loud country music and laughing. Jim realized they must have been let out of school early after finals. The beat-up truck passed them quickly, with the teens not giving the family an extra look. The kids were apparently too absorbed in each other and their freedom.

A mile past the farm entrance, Jack slowed, and they began looking for the place Pete had shown them on the map. Finally, they came to a small, worn-out driveway that led to the back of the Hoke barn. It was worn-out but not recently used. The grass rising in the middle of the lane was growing high. It made a sound as it brushed the underside of the RV while they drove slowly along the path.

It felt like a long drive since they were exposed to the road for a few minutes, but quickly they were hidden by trees. The dark green woods enveloped them and they drove in silence. Before them, a large barn structure grew as they approached. It was just as Jim would have imagined, with red wood and white trim. It looked newer than he would have thought, so they must have replaced an older structure fairly recently in relative terms. The RV would easily fit inside.

They drove up to the front and stopped before the door. Pete's head popped out from the left side of the barn, and he moved to open the large doors. Jack drove in and parked. They all immediately hopped out of the RV to check out their surroundings. Jim noticed that the inside of the barn was in better shape than the outside, which had weathered a bit. It was beautiful. There were stalls for large animals, a high ceiling with windows that let in a lot of light, and what Jim thought of as a lounge area that had a table and chairs, some cupboards, and a full bathroom. It wasn't fancy, but it was very nice. They wouldn't be able to plug their RV in for electricity, but they had water and a bathroom in the barn. It would work for a few days if needed.

Jilly immediately set herself up in one of the stalls, pretending to be a horse. She was galloping around and making neighing noises. Charlie was watching her like she had lost her mind at first, but he quickly became amused and smiled. Karen checked out the bathroom and proclaimed it clean. The girls were always looking for the best bathrooms when they traveled. Apparently this one was okay.

"You guys good for now?" Pete asked.

"Yeah. Thanks a lot," Jack answered.

"Hey, nobody's really talking about things at Mel's, but there was a table of guys in the back who were talkin' all quiet. Who knows. Give us a call if you need anything. We'll bring you guys more food tomorrow. Just make a list, Shawna said."

"Thanks," Jack said, and Pete was off.

After a little time getting settled, the family quietly left the barn and entered the woods. They were going in search of the family. Charlie took the lead and stayed thirty feet in front of them. He was constantly sniffing and stopping to listen. They walked on for a very long time, longer than they had before. Jim noticed the woods were getting thicker. The area to the front of the property was obviously where the cows had mostly grazed when they had lived there. Where the bigfoot family lived before, more toward the middle of the property, the dense woods had less underbrush but still more than the front of the property. Back here, though, was untouched. The trees were tall, creating a dark canopy that shut out much of the sunlight. There was brush of medium height, yaupons, and other plants Jim didn't recognize, but they were hard to move through.

It was slow going, but they kept at it. In front of them, Charlie was working hard to track Scar and his family, but it looked like even he was having a hard time. They were coming at the site from the other side, more toward the back of the property, but Jim noticed that they were veering off from where they had imagined the family would hide. Charlie stopped in front of them and let out a quiet yelping sound. It was actually pretty loud, but quiet for

Charlie, because Jim knew Charlie could be much louder than that. Still, it wasn't loud enough that everyone within a short distance would hear it. They all held their breath and waited patiently for an answer but none came.

Jim was worried. Had they been killed? Captured? Had they left the area entirely?

They began moving again when they finally heard a small yelp to their right. It was from deeper within the property. Visualizing the map, Jim knew that the sound came from the far edge of the Hoke property. Behind the property on that side was another large hunk of land that belonged to someone else, but since it was a whole lot of nothing, they would be safe there.

Charlie finally stopped and grew rigid. He was listening ahead and to the right. Jim and his family stopped and waited. Charlie turned to them and motioned for them to stay, with the universal sign of holding up his huge hand. Jim was anxious. It was hard to wait and not know what was going on. He disappeared in the thick woods before them, so they all relaxed and sat down to wait.

It was quite a while before Charlie came back to them. Jim figured either the family was far away, or they had been having a conversation about recent events and, perhaps, the Thomas' involvement. Either way, Charlie looked okay and motioned them to follow. They walked with him quite a ways away. When they arrived, it was obvious that the family was worried about seeing them again.

Scar was standing in front of his family. The mother holding her baby, and the boy was hiding behind her legs, peaking out with round eyes.

Charlie walked forward and greeted them again. Scar nodded at Charlie, but he kept his eyes on the approaching family.

"Hello," Jack said. Karen echoed his greeting.

Scar stood there, staring, then finally made an almost imperceptible nod and moved aside. Karen peeled Jilly off her hand, and

Jim took over holding her other hand. She then walked straight up to the baby, with determination and confidence. As she did, she pulled out her bottle of antibiotics. The mother's rigid stance softened, and she looked relieved. The baby was more active and lively than Jim had seen her. She was squirming in her mother's arms and making soft noises. Karen deftly got the antibiotics in the wriggling baby's mouth and rubbed her little face.

Jim felt like they were worried about his family putting them in danger. And they were right. While they hadn't brought the TV crew there, they had brought Charlie, and that's who was caught on camera. However, Scar probably would have tried to scare them off anyway, so maybe it all would have happened even if Jim and his family hadn't been there. They would never know, but he couldn't help but feel mostly responsible for their current situation.

"I'm sorry," he said, "Sorry for bringing any danger to you if we did." He was speaking directly to Scar and the mother. He knew they didn't understand his words, but he hoped they understood that he felt bad and was sorry.

Charlie was standing next to Scar and nodded to him. They all looked at Scar. He was quiet and still. Finally, he walked up to Jim and raised a large, hairy arm. The pats Scar gave his shoulder nearly knocked Jim over, but he was so glad to receive them. Scar was okay.

They didn't stay long. Only a few minutes, but it was a good visit. When it was time, Charlie led them back the way they had come. Everyone was on the lookout for cameras or people, but nothing out of the ordinary was seen.

Dinner was sandwiches and chips. They couldn't use the generator in the barn, so they didn't have a microwave or oven, and they didn't want to make a fire outside. They were being as stealthy as possible.

Shawna called after dinner. Things were picking up in town. That evening at Mel's, there was a large commotion. It seemed that word was spreading, and it was a good thing that they had moved the RV, because people wanted to go talk to them about what they had seen.

Apparently, the people were fairly evenly split into three groups. There were those who were excited and wanted to help protect the bigfoot and saw it as a positive opportunity for the town; those who were afraid and wanted to get rid of it; and those who didn't believe a word of anything regarding bigfoot. No matter what anyone believed, Charlie's existence was no longer secret.

Neither was the family's involvement.

That night, they opened the windows of the RV since they couldn't use their air conditioner. Even with the barn doors closed, they could hear the loud sounds of the woods. Crickets, cicadas, frogs, and who knew what else were singing their nightly songs. It made a pleasant white noise to fall asleep to.

CHAPTER NINETEEN
Brewing Storm

THEY SPENT A couple of days like this, enjoying the secret nature of their stay and taking care of the bigfoot family as best as they could.

One morning brought dark clouds and storms. The wind had picked up and was blowing leaves and other debris around. Inside the barn, Jim was cozy. They had the lights on and had set up enough chairs around the table that they moved into the middle of the barn, in front of the RV. Breakfast was frozen waffles. They were able to plug the toaster into the wall in the lounge, so they had a nice breakfast. Jilly had taken Charlie to a stall next to them to play with some of her toys. Charlie had seemed anxious at first, but with the growing threat of a nasty storm, he had calmed down and was now curled up in a corner of the stall, resting his head. His eyes were lazily watching Jilly move her ponies around the stall. Jim thought he had the right idea: rest while you can.

The small door just off the lounge area slammed open, the wind ripping it from Shawna's hand as she entered. Pete and Larry tumbled in after her.

"Geez, that wind is a killer," Shawna said.

"No kidding," Pete agreed. "Sky looks like something out of *Twister.*"

Larry nervously licked his lips and then asked, "So does that mean you won't be going to see the family this morning?"

The man never seemed to calm down. Jim thought he must be constantly exhausted.

Karen answered. "We'll have to wait a little bit. It's quite a hike in that weather."

"Sure, sure," Shawna said, taking a seat at the table next to Karen. "So, can we come?"

Karen looked at her with pursed lips. "I'd like to say yes, but I'm not sure how they would react to all of you."

"Maybe if you all say we're okay, and Charlie says we're okay, they'll be okay with us," Larry offered.

"We can try," was all Karen would say.

Pete poked his head over the stall and grinned. "I wanna see the big guy."

Jim laughed. "I think Charlie's been missing sleep. He's been so excited to see other bigfoot."

Shawna's head popped up. "Do they speak to each other?"

"Well, yeah," Jim answered. "They have some sort of language. It sounds funny. Kinda like a gurgly, mumbly noise. I can't explain it." He laughed self-consciously, his face reddening.

"That's it," Jack agreed. "It's fascinating to listen to them talk and watch it. There are a lot more gestures involved than with humans. It seems as though they use more body language and tone."

Shawna shifted in her seat. "There aren't too many of them. Let's assume they haven't had a way to communicate over large distances. Safe, right? Well then how would these two be able to communicate? Would they know the same language? Is it enough of a language to even really learn or is it just, like, some rudimentary words and the rest is just, like, conveyed on the spot, through trial and error?"

"Not sure," Jim said. "We sort of assumed the third one, sort of. Like maybe they had a language a long time ago, but now it's kind of like an ancient language that they sort of know parts to. I don't know."

Shawna stood up quickly and started pacing. She ran her hands through her hair. "This is amazing. I can't even imagine something like that. What are they? They're capable of language. That's incredible in itself. They're bipedal. They're capable of more complex stuff than other apes. They can use primitive tools, they've never had a body found, they stay well hidden. Are they like a primitive human? Are they just a super ape? We would need DNA to figure things out."

Her rant was making Jim nervous. This is the kind of excitement that is great but frightening, too.

"Dude," Pete said. He was looking at Shawna with a "calm down" look.

"Oh right. I know, I'm getting too carried away. I mean, I understand the problem with going public with all of this, but I'm just saying it's fascinating."

"Good," Jack said.

"So, what do you think those guys were after? The ones who hunted Charlie. The Mortons," Jim asked.

Shawna shook her head like she had no idea. "I guess they wanted to get in on any money that might come with finding proof. Especially a body."

Everyone nodded.

Jim remembered his conversation with Mr. Walker and added, "I asked Mr. Walker about them in Mel's the other day. They always sit in there, looking mean and staring at us. He said they're another old family here. They started the town with the Hokes and whoever else. So they wanted Hoke's land and Hoke never gave in. Now that he's gone, they've been trying to get it again, and he says they're really interested in what you guys have been doing there, you know, with the bigfoot hunting."

Nobody had heard that yet. Jack said, "Seems they may feel like the bigfoot belongs to them, in a way."

"Oh, and he said they're greedy."

"Well there you go," Pete said. "Money, money, money."

"They're huge hunters, too," Larry cut in. "We went to interview them at one of their houses, and they have heads up all over the place. Big stuff, too. I understand hunting, but this is a different situation we're talking about. More about show than real hunting."

Jim agreed.

They talked for a while longer, telling stories, sharing ideas. Lunchtime rolled around, and they made sandwiches again. Jim looked at the sandwich items and felt like he couldn't eat another sandwich today. He went to the RV to rummage through the cupboards for other snacks. He found a pack of peanut butter crackers and some Oreos. Not the healthiest, but at least the thought of those wasn't making him sick. He felt the RV rock as someone heavy stepped up through the open door.

Charlie.

"Hey, Charlie," Jim greeted him. His face looked sleepy, and his hair was ruffled from lying down.

Charlie looked at him, then saw his Oreos. Charlie typically wasn't big on sweets, but Oreos were some of his favorite treats. Jim opened the package and split them with him. They stood, munching on cookies. Jim's mind was on the new bigfoot family and Charlie. Would they be okay? Would Charlie want to stay with them? He couldn't imagine life without Charlie now.

Somehow sensing his worry, Charlie put his heavy arm around Jim's shoulders and squeezed. This simple act soothed Jim's worries, and he felt like everything would be okay.

Jim heard Pete's voice from outside. "Hey, the rain's letting up. You going to see the family?" Jim looked at Charlie once more, then brushed by him to join the others in the barn. He heard his dad answer, "Yes, we have to give the baby its medicine."

"I suppose it's too early for us to join?" Shawna half stated, half asked.

Karen spoke up. "I think so. Let's take things sort of slowly."

Shawna's face was full of disappointment, but she smiled and nodded. "We'll get some supplies for you guys and see if we can talk the Mortons into believing they saw something else."

CHAPTER TWENTY
Stolen

THE THOMAS FAMILY got ready to hike out. Karen passed out the rain ponchos and rubber boots. Jilly was mad that she couldn't wear her bright pink boots, but they didn't want to draw any unwanted attention.

While they prepared, Shawna, Pete, and Larry all gathered around Charlie. They were each asking questions that they knew he couldn't answer and trying to get him to say their names. Charlie looked to Jim for help, but Jim could only shrug. He didn't know what to tell him.

When they were ready, the two groups parted ways, with the Thomas family heading out with Charlie to meet the family. After a few minutes, Jim was enjoying their walk. The ground was mushy and water was still dropping from the leaves all around them. The sky was gray. It was a cozy day, and the woods enveloping them gave the day a green warmth that was comforting to Jim. He felt at home.

They had been walking for a while when they started hearing noises in the distance. They sounded like a large animal moving through the woods. The sounds were coming from different places here and there. It was like something moving erratically through the brush. Jim's mind immediately went to a frightened deer. While they were graceful and could be quiet, when they were afraid, they moved with reckless abandon and crashed through the woods, away from danger. He was wondering what it was doing, when he heard a loud cry. It was an agonizing sound, one full of fear and misery.

And it wasn't a deer.

Charlie's body tensed, and his eyes widened. Something was scaring him, too. Suddenly, he charged forward through the trees and disappeared, leaving Jim and his family to wonder what was happening and huddle together in worry.

A nearing crashing sound let them know that Charlie was returning. At least Jim hoped it was Charlie. He finally saw Charlie's reddish brown hair step out from behind a tree at a running pace. He was hurrying toward them with a hard look on his face, eyes determined, jaw set. Scar was at his heels.

They stopped before the family, both breathing hard. Scar's eyes were wild, and his head was constantly swiveling around. He looked like an animal that had lost all control of a situation. He looked cornered and scared.

He looked wild.

"What's going on?" Jack asked.

Charlie answered his questioning tone by pointing at Scar, and then pointing at Jilly, and shaking his head.

"What's wrong with me?" Jilly asked, horrified. She didn't realize Charlie wasn't actually referring to her.

"Nothing, honey. Charlie's trying to tell us something about one of Scar's kids," Karen answered.

She was right. Charlie had pointed at Jilly, probably indicating that something had happened to Scar's own daughter, the infant.

But what?

Jim grabbed Charlie's thick forearm and forced him to look at him. "What happened? Is she sick?" He put a hand on his stomach and mimed being ill. Charlie narrowed his eyes and then shook his head. Jim asked the question that he was most afraid of getting the answer to. "Did someone take her?" He wasn't sure how to convey this message but did the best he could with gesturing. He pointed at Jilly and then away, and raised his arms, as if asking where she went. It worked, because Charlie hesitantly nodded.

Scar let out an anguished wail and patted Charlie's shoulder impatiently. Charlie looked at him and then gestured to the family to follow. They went racing through the woods. Jack had to pick up Jilly, who was having trouble keeping up. Twigs, leaves, and branches all smacked at them. Thorns grabbed their clothes and exposed skin, but they kept moving. Finally, they came to a halt. Scar made a chuffing sound, and the mother moved forward from her hiding place behind a stand of trees. Horrifyingly, Jim realized she was alone.

The boy was gone, too.

She looked positively broken. Her eyes were red and pinched together with worry. Jim felt so badly for her.

Scar pointed to a spot, and Charlie began sniffing. He began walking and sniffing, seeming to follow his nose. They all followed him. He walked on, stopping here and there to sniff and listen. Finally, he broke into a run, and they had a hard time keeping up. Jim had picked up Jilly to give Jack a rest, but he was having a hard time moving with her on his back. Still, he didn't dare slow or stop.

After what felt like an hour, they broke through the treeline. A barbwire fence stood about twenty feet away, separating the Hoke's land from another piece of land. Jim recognized the area. It was near the back of the Hoke property, where they had visited the days before while investigating with the TV crew. Someone else owned the land on the other side, and Jim had a sneaking suspicion that the Mortons owned it. Whoever had taken the boy and infant had come that way.

Jim knew they had to call Shawna. They needed her help.

Scar stood just inside the treeline, with tears in his eyes. He looked destroyed. In contrast, Charlie looked like Jim had never seen him before. He looked scary. His eyes were drawn into a fiery glare. He was oddly calm, but he looked determined and tensed for action. Jim was surprised at the depth of his anger.

He turned swiftly on his heel and headed back into the woods. It took a while to get back to the barn, but they hurried as best as they could. Little was said. They all knew what had happened. The Mortons had come back and stolen the little ones somehow. Jim found it hard to believe. The bigfoot family had always been so cautious and well hidden. How had those people been able to get their hands on the little ones?

Along the way, they picked the mother up. She and Scar began following them back to the barn, their shoulders drooping in despair. Jim glanced back a couple of times to see Scar putting a comforting hand on her hand or shoulder. It was odd to see them acting so human about this. He tried to imagine gorillas or other apes showing such affection. He sort of could, but this was different somehow. Jilly kept asking quiet questions, and Jim did his best to answer. At one point, he heard her crying softly into the back of his neck. She was scared.

As they walked, Jim heard Jack make a phone call to Shawna. He heard him relay what had happened and ask her and the guys to try to find out what they could. They were on the case.

Jim was relieved to have other people who could help them, but he still felt like their situation was almost hopeless. He hated thinking that way, but he did. He just couldn't see this staying quiet, especially in this small town. Word would spread like wildfire to the ends of the earth.

When they made it to the barn, Scar and the mother stopped outside. They had never been inside a building before, and Jim could sense their fear and discomfort. He watched Scar's eyes move over the structure, and then he finally gave his head a shake and moved forward, taking the mother with him. They entered the barn, and Charlie took them to a corner and got them situated.

Jack grabbed his car keys and started for the Jeep.

"Where are you going?" Karen asked. "We're supposed to be keeping a low profile."

"I can't just sit here. I have to move, do something."

"Jack, I understand what you're feeling, but we need to be smart about this. For them and for our family."

Jack was breathing hard and let out a deep breath. He was seething. Jim was furious, too, but he was more scared than anything. He looked at Charlie. There was a calm, determined look on his face. Jim had never seen him look like that before. He thought back to when he first had met Charlie and realized that Charlie had grown up. He was a young bigfoot, but in a short amount of time, he had matured. Jim could see that Charlie could take care of himself.

Jack's phone rang with its old-timey telephone ringtone blaring in the anxious quiet of the barn. Scar and the mother both jumped at the harsh sound. Jack answered. He listened for a minute and then said, "See you in a few," and hung up.

"They're heading over now. They say they have information." He stopped pacing and looked around, then he finally sat down, obviously relenting to the fact that they couldn't do anything just yet. The sag in his body said it all.

Karen busied herself by taking care of Jilly and then getting food and water for everybody. She presented the bigfoot couple with their own plates of food. They stared at them with big eyes, and after some prodding from Charlie, they took the plates and began eating. Jim watched them inspect the whole set-up. Despite the seriousness of the situation, Jim had to smile.

There was a knock on the door, and then Shawna opened it. She began to enter the barn and froze. The sight of the two new bigfoot had paralyzed her for a moment, but she quickly recovered. Pete and Larry both took turns freezing in surprise, but everyone was finally inside.

"You've got to be kidding me," Shawna finally said. Her face broke into a grin. Pete started laughing and smiling. Larry stared, mouth hanging open.

Scar and the mother were huddled together in their corner, shrinking away from the newcomers. Scar stood in front of the mother, protecting her unnecessarily. Jim felt for them. Though they had nothing to fear from the humans, they couldn't help it.

"What in the world is happening?" Shawna asked.

"You tell us. What did you find out?" Jack asked.

Shawna's face turned serious, getting back to the somber business at hand. "We've been invited to see, what did they call it, 'the find of a lifetime' by our old friends, the Mortons."

Jim had known that's what had happened, but he had still been hoping that somehow it wasn't true.

This wasn't good.

"Where are they?" Karen asked.

"Don't know yet. They say they'll call us with a location if we're serious about it, and we have to meet one of them and be taken there."

Pete snorted. "Probably blindfolded."

Jim figured he was right. But how many people knew?

"What about other people? Is everyone talking about it?" he asked.

Shawna tilted her head in a way to show she was thinking. "There seemed to be a slight buzz going on around town, especially at Mel's. Can't say for sure, but I'd bet word's getting out."

Jim's heart sank. This was a nightmare.

"What should we do?" Larry asked nervously. His thin arms were crossed in front of his chest, and he still blinked continuously, but he was getting more comfortable around them.

Nobody had an answer. Everyone looked around at each other, but nobody said anything. This was uncharted territory.

Jim let his eyes drop and sat quietly for a moment. He felt a familiar sense of dread and worry. They had been in a similar situation before, but this time felt even more desperate, more hopeless. He couldn't let himself feel that way, though. To feel that way would be to give up.

"So they should go and see what information they can get," he said to his parents. "Then we'll make a plan from there."

Jack's face stayed tight. Jim knew it wasn't much of a plan, but they needed information. "That's a start."

Shawna made the call, and they planned to meet in an hour. The crew would go to the same store where Jim had first met the three crew members, and a car would take them from there. Over the next forty-five minutes, they discussed what might happen and tried to plan for all contingencies. Really, they couldn't do much until they knew what they were up against.

Jim realized that he was hearing the quiet humming of Jilly's small voice in the background and turned to see her talking quietly to Scar and the mother. She was trying to put a blanket on them and give them some cups of water, but they just weren't sure what she was doing. Charlie watched from his seat along the wall of a stall, with an amused smile on his face.

"Are we going to try to steal them out of there at some point?" Larry asked with a slight tremor in his voice. Jim turned to look at him. Despite his voice, he had a determined glint in his eyes. Speaking up in front of a group of people must be hard for him, but he looked ready for action.

"Dude, of course. We can't leave them there," Pete said. He looked at everyone and nodded in a sort of "Right?" manner.

Karen answered. "We'll do whatever we can."

Jim understood that she was being cautiously realistic, but he wished she sounded more confident. With nothing left to do, Jim walked to the other side of the barn and opened one of the windows. He could hear crickets, cicadas, and other sounds in the woods. It was a beautiful day out there now.

A shuffling sound behind him drew his attention from the scene outside. Shawna had walked up beside him and was looking out the window. Her dark eyes took in the view, and her face softened. Jim noticed there were gold flecks in her brown eyes, and the sunlight made them shine.

"Pretty, huh?" she asked in a soft voice.

"Oh yeah. It's always great in the country."

She pulled her eyes away from the scene, but it looked like it was difficult for her; her eyes were the last to turn to him. Jim was slightly breathless for a moment with her attention fully on him, but he finally remembered to breathe again.

"You're quite a guy, Jim. Your whole family is great, really. I bet this is tough for you, though."

Jim's cheeks felt hot with the compliment. "Thanks. Yeah, it's kinda tough, but it's awesome."

She smiled and looked back outside.

"Why did you help us?" He knew she had said before, but he wanted more of an explanation.

She blinked and looked at him, took a deep breath. "Well, I guess I felt stupid."

"Huh?"

"You can't tell anyone, but I didn't truly believe. I mean, I heard the stories, I figured there could possibly be something to them, but still, I didn't really think there was something like them out there. And if there was, I didn't think it would be so likeable."

Jim laughed. Charlie was likeable. In fact, he was amazing.

"So when I saw Charlie, I was stunned. Then when I saw him interacting with you guys, I felt like an idiot. Then I look over and see these guys wanting to kill him. It just didn't feel right. I'm such an animal lover, so I couldn't watch that happen." She laughed a little uncomfortably at that.

Jim was quiet for a moment.

"What about Pete and Larry?"

She grinned while looking out the window. A hawk was making circles above, hunting for prey. She was watching its flight.

"Pete's been my friend for years. I think he kinda has a crush on me and would do whatever I asked, but he really does love shooting videos and photography. Larry, we met him at school. He's a nice guy. Quiet but nice. He wants to get into making movies. To be honest, we know nothing about bigfoot stuff. I've done some research, sure, but we're not like those other guys who do this full time and professionally. They probably laugh at our ridiculousness. We just thought it would be fun and a way to kinda get some experience in our areas of interest, and maybe get a bit famous." She ended with a wink at him, then her eyes turned back to the scenery.

"Do you want to make movies, too?"

Her eyes found him again. Now she looked uncomfortable. "I thought I did." She turned and leaned with her back against the window, the sun lighting up her hair from behind. "I thought it would be fun and people told me I should go get on TV and stuff, but I've discovered I'm really a nerd," she said with a laugh. "I took a lot of biology courses before I decided on journalism, but I've really gotten into the research, and I like going out and trying to collect evidence. I love biology, and I'm really considering going back to school for my biology degree or something like that. Now that I've met Charlie, I'd like to do some conservation work or something."

Jim smiled back at her. "That's great. You should do that if you want to."

"Thanks. We'll see. Maybe I could get my own science show. What do ya think?" She laughed loudly this time, and he laughed with her. It was nice to be happy for a short time.

"Shawna," Pete called.

"Yeah?" she answered. She looked at Jim and motioned with her head for him to follow her back to the group. They walked up to the table, where the others were gathered. Jack had a map spread over the table and was showing Pete and Larry the area.

"Jack's showing us the layout so we can know where we are when we go meet these bozos," Pete said.

"Hopefully," Larry added.

"That's a good idea," Shawna agreed.

They spent a while going over the map and possible scenarios, but everyone finally fell quiet. There was a quietly nervous buzz in the room. Jim kept looking at Scar and the mother, who were staying really quiet, like animals do when they're trying not to be noticed. Charlie was sticking close to them. Jilly was sitting cross-legged on a blanket on the floor, quietly watching the newcomers, her chin in her hands. She was unusually still.

The phone rang and everyone jumped. Shawna answered, sounding very cool, not a bit anxious. She listened for a moment and then said, "Okay." She stood.

It was time.

Jim and his family walked Shawna, Pete, and Larry out to their van and wished them good luck. As they drove away, Jim wished he could go with them, but he knew he would just have to be patient.

CHAPTER TWENTY-ONE
Options

THE TIME PASSED slowly, but Jim busied himself with trying to think of ways to help the two little ones when they found out where they were. His mind kept getting more and more elaborate with the rescue plans. He started imagining himself going in there Arnold Schwarzenegger-style, and he had to shake his head to get back to reality.

An engine could be heard in the distance, and Jim could quickly tell that it was nearing. He shot up subconsciously and went to the window. It was dark out now, and all he could see was the blinding gleam of approaching headlights. Finally, the bulky shape of the van could be seen, and he anxiously went to the door.

Shawna came through first. Her eyes were flashing, and her cheeks were flushed.

"I can't believe them! They're horrible!"

"What happened?" Karen asked.

The crew walked in, and Pete sat down heavily. Larry looked extra anxious and nervous, so he stood against the wall, his arms crossed in front of his chest. Shawna couldn't sit. She looked too upset. Instead, she paced around the room in random routes.

"Well, first of all, they *did* blindfold us. Can you believe it? Blindfolded!"

Pete snorted.

"Then they took us to what I'm fairly certain was the same house we went to before," Shawna continued. "There was this certain dip in their driveway that we felt again tonight. But, of course, they said we were in some other place and that nobody around here knew about it. It was a barn or some other building. We were taken into this little room that had a window into another room. They were in there, the little ones."

"It was so sad, dude!" Pete interjected.

"Yeah, it was," Shawna agreed. Their eyes were serious and sad as they reflected on what they had seen. All three of them looked down for a moment, then Shawna continued. "So they tell us they have a contract we have to sign, looked like something they typed up, and they say we can have exclusive access to them, and they get seventy percent of what we can sell them for."

Pete snorted again.

"They also want to sell access to scientists first, then the public. It'll be like a zoo exhibit. Can you believe that?" She stole a look at Scar and the mother, then lowered her voice. "They're also prepared to kill the older one and sell it to the highest bidder. They think a scientist or some group will want the body for study. Only dead, though. They don't want to sell one alive. Apparently they think they're worth more alive but have no problem getting money for the body."

"They said that?" Karen barked out. She was aghast.

"They had it all spelled right out in their contract," Larry answered.

"They really are greedy," Jim muttered.

"Does anyone else know about this?" Karen asked.

"Not sure," Shawna replied. "They didn't say, but don't people like that tell everyone in town?"

"Not necessarily," Jack said. "These guys seem different. More secretive. And greedy, like Jim said."

Pete looked around and rocked back in his chair. "So, uh, what do we do?"

Silence settled on the group. Everyone was lost in thought.

Jack broke the silence. "We've done something like this before. This is a bit different, though. We're strangers here."

Shawna rolled her eyes like "of course," and nodded her head. "Yeah, so you guys are experts at breaking these guys out of enemy strongholds, too? What else can you do?"

Karen laughed. "We may have had a sort of similar situation with Charlie last year. But that's for another time. Right now we need to figure this out. How many people are involved?"

"Looked like just the two of them so far. We didn't see anyone else or hear anyone else."

"Let's assume they're at the house you guys went to before. What's the situation like?" Jack asked.

They were getting on a roll.

"Well, it's kind of typical country. Decent-sized house. One story. Long driveway, lots of trees. They have a big barn that you can't really see from the road. But out back, it's a big, big building. It's not really a barn, though, because they say they don't have animals. It looks more like a big place for, like, their tractor, 4-wheelers, whatever else they may have. Wouldn't you guys say?"

Pete and Larry nodded in agreement. Pete said, "It was more like one of those big warehouse things."

Jack nodded. "Any security?"

"Not that we saw," Larry answered.

Jim noticed that he was speaking up more often now.

"Okay." Jack stood and began pacing. "How did you guys leave things?"

Shawna answered. "We tried to play it cool and say we were going to get some things and come back, but they wanted us to sign the contract right then. I just couldn't. I said we had to think about it. They said it was then or never."

"So they ended it?"

"I guess. They said it was then or never, we said we had to think about it, then they said they'd take us home, and that was that."

"Okay." Jack began pacing again.

"Guys, I think we have to act fast, before they get some other TV station in here or kill one of them or something," Pete said. Jim thought he was starting to sound panicked.

"We're going to do what we can, but we have to be smart," Karen said. Apparently sensing the same thing Jim had sensed, she used a soothing tone.

They spent the next couple of hours discussing different strategies. Everything sounded weak and impossible. It was getting very late. Jilly had fallen asleep on her little blanket, and Charlie had picked her up and followed Karen to the RV to put her in her soft bed. He came back and made a pallet for himself and helped Scar and the mother with their own little beds in a stall.

Shawna and the guys got sleeping bags from their van and set up in another stall. Everyone quickly got ready for sleep and fell into bed.

Jim felt so tired he thought he could sleep for days. At the same time, he wanted to get up as soon as possible and get to work. As he got ready for bed, which included the bare minimum since he was so tired, he thought about the poor captured bigfoot children. They had to be so confused and terrified. The only people they had ever been in contact with were Jim and his family, who had treated them very well. Now they were in the hands of the Mortons.

It was a nightmare. They had to be saved.

Jim fell asleep with the faces of each of the children floating through his mind.

CHAPTER TWENTY-TWO
Showtime

A POUNDING ON the RV door woke Jim. It felt like he had only been asleep for maybe a minute, but it had actually been about six hours, according to his phone. Jack came padding sleepily through the RV and answered the door. As usual, he was the only one able to get up and think quickly with little sleep, and only seconds after waking up.

Beyond Jack, Jim heard Pete's voice. He sounded breathless. "Hey, dude. We got a phone call. They're still peddling their little sideshow and want our help. Looks like they want to debut them here in town. Today."

Jim heard a quiet curse from Jack. The door closed, and Jack turned around. "Everyone up. It's going to be a bad day."

Jim popped up from the bed and grabbed some clothes from his bag.

Karen came into the room, rubbing her eyes. "What did he say?"

"They're going to show the kids to the town today," Jack answered grimly.

"They're not wasting any time."

Jim went to the bathroom to get ready. Everyone was whirling around as they rushed to face the day. In a matter of minutes, they were out the door, still half asleep. Jilly was rubbing her eyes and walking stiffly, but to her credit, she was up and not complaining.

"Hey, guys," Shawna greeted them. Jim could smell coffee and toast. Charlie was sitting with Scar and the mother, who were watching the proceedings with tight faces. They knew something was happening. "Didn't waste any time, eh?"

"What did they say, exactly?" Karen asked.

"Well, they said that they're going to be showing the two kids in town and that we could still be the exclusive news crew. They don't want anyone taking pictures or video without their consent, and they're not consenting. Asked us since we have a bit of a following and some interest in this area. And we're here. But that'll be the extent of our involvement. Guess we missed out on the big deal yesterday."

"Boo hoo," Pete said, rolling his eyes.

"Where are they going to be?" Jim asked.

"Guess," Larry quipped. His first word of the day.

"Mel's, huh?" Jim said. Larry nodded, and Pete did the finger gun gesture like, "You got it." He said, "Everything happens there."

"What time?" Jack asked.

"A couple of hours," Pete answered. "Can we stop it before it happens? Because we can't make those people unsee those guys. Word will be out after that."

Jack took a deep breath and exhaled sharply. "I don't see how."

That took the wind out of everyone's sails. What had felt like an impromptu rescue mission was now just preparation to go gawk and see how everyone else reacted. It felt like a hopeless situation, and Jim hated it.

"Can we stop the guys?" he asked. "Can we talk them into waiting for some reason?"

Shawna answered this one. "Doubt it. They're not the reasonable type."

A chirping sound made everyone jump. Shawna reached for her pocket and pulled out her phone. "Shawna Pepper."

She listened for a moment and said, "Thanks," then hung up. "That was Mr. Walker. He said people are gathering at Mel's." At their confused expressions, she added, "I asked him to call if anything unusual happened."

Jim was surprised that he would call them. "How does he really know you guys? Didn't you just interview him?"

"Yeah, well, the other night we all were talking about everything going on around here," she started speaking faster after seeing the Thomas' alarmed reactions, "just the sightings, and then there were the rumblings about the Mortons seeing something and shooting at it. Nothing beyond that. But anyway, Mr. Walker and his family were talking about their encounter again, and how they wanted to help him and just leave him alone. We shared that sentiment, and they said they would let us know if anything was happening and asked us to do the same."

"That's great. So we have at least a couple of allies," Jim said. The thought of Eva helping them if she could made Jim smile. He felt a tingle of happiness surge through him.

"Yep, but what good is that actually going to do us after today?" Shawna asked.

They got ready to leave.

Jim and his mom made sure Charlie and the others were set with food, water, and blankets. Charlie looked Jim in the eyes, and Jim knew he was worried, but he could also feel the confidence Charlie had in him and his family. It made Jim feel great and terrible at the same time. While they had helped Charlie before, they couldn't do anything now.

Piling into their vehicles, the two groups were silent. Jim noticed the day was gray with a brewing storm. It felt like an ominous warning. The sky was full of swirling gray clouds that seemed to be bringing tense energy to the day. It mirrored his mood.

The drive there took an extra long time, but Jim realized that it was probably just because he was anxious and worried. It was funny how roads seemed longer and almost unfamiliar when you were trying to get somewhere fast.

Finally, he could see the small, square building growing nearer. The parking lot was packed, and there were people filing in, and small groups standing behind their cars and trucks. There was a definite buzz in the air as they pulled into a space in front of the hardware store nearby. Jim got out and saw Pete pulling the van into a space a few cars down from them. They got out and joined the family.

It was a circus.

Jim realized that it was Saturday morning, so nobody was really working and nobody was in school. In a small town like Bisby, word traveled fast, and everyone wanted to see the big surprise. Jim looked at Jack, and then they both stepped into the street. Looking around, he realized that most people were dressed in royal blue and white—the high school team colors. He looked at the cars and trucks parked and driving along, all had decorations for the baseball team. Apparently there was a big game today, and they were playing the Mustangs, whoever they were.

Terrible timing.

Everyone was in town already, getting geared up for the game. They were probably having breakfast and visiting with each other, so adding a big show like the Mortons' big reveal was just further draw. They would have a huge crowd.

As they approached, Jim could see some people that he sort of recognized from Mel's spot them and start whispering. They all must have thought Jim and his family were long gone. Well, there would be two surprises today.

The girl who had been running the to-go station the first night they had arrived was standing at the doorway, yelling something. As they got nearer, Jim could hear her.

"Everybody line up! You gotta have a ticket to get in! Get your tickets over there from Junior!" She was pointing at the corner of the building where a burly young man was holding a large reel of tickets and taking money. He looked like he was probably on the school's wrestling team. And the football team, the baseball team, probably basketball, and any other athletic team they had. He probably wrestled livestock on a daily basis, too, because his arms were huge. Nobody was arguing with him, and everyone was being orderly.

Despite the large number of people outside, Jim noticed that there was a large group that wasn't buying tickets. Apparently they didn't want to pay to see something when they didn't have even a clue of what it was.

Jim looked at his parents. Jack raised his eyebrows, and Karen nodded.

They got in line.

"We're going to make the call," Shawna said, and the three of them stepped aside.

Jim saw Shawna on the phone. She hung up after only seconds and motioned the guys to follow her. They went to the girl at the door, who opened it for them. They disappeared inside.

Jim wished he could be in there and see what was happening. He looked up and down the line; too many people were looking right back at him. Fortunately, nobody said a word, but there were plenty of whispers.

"There you are," came a voice from behind him.

Jim turned to see Mr. Walker and Eva standing before him.

"Somehow figured y'all would be here."

He took Jack and Jim's hands in a firm shake and nodded to Karen and Jilly.

"What's going on, do you think?" Jack asked him.

Jim stole a look at Eva again, and she mouthed "hi" to him. He returned the greeting and felt his face get hot.

"We figure they think they caught him, whatever he is."

Jack grimaced. "That's what we were thinking."

"There've been hoaxes like this before," Eva said. "They're always hoaxes. Hopefully this one is, too."

Jim hoped that people did think it was somehow a hoax. But really, once they saw these guys, there would be no doubt.

Mr. Walker looked up and then said, "We better get in line. It's moving pretty quickly." Eva waved bye, and they disappeared near the end of the line.

Jim and his family were finally able to buy tickets from Junior, who looked pleased with the power his job gave him, however temporary and slight. He flexed his arms every time he tore a ticket off the reel and looked around to make sure people were seeing his importance.

The line was moving quickly. They were handing their tickets over to the girl in no time and crossed the threshold.

The place was filling up.

Jim saw that they had moved some tables to create a space near the back of the diner, where there was a sort of make-shift stage. They had many more chairs than he was used to seeing in there, too. Most were folding chairs. Jim looked out over the sea of blue and white. It looked like a sporting event. Shawna, Pete, and Larry were nowhere to be seen.

Jim and his family moved to the far side of the diner and slipped toward the back, along the wall. Karen and Jilly snagged a couple of chairs on the end of the second-to-front row, and Jim and Jack stood beside them against the wall.

Now they waited.

Within minutes, the place was full, and the wave of people entering became a trickle. Finally, the girl came inside with Junior and shut the door.

It was showtime.

Junior went to the back of the diner, looking like he was very important, with a puffed up chest, and then disappeared through a door. After a couple of minutes, he reappeared and claimed a spot next to the to-go girl, who practically swooned when she saw him take up a casual pose beside her.

Jim turned back to the stage and saw that Shawna, Pete, and Larry had apparently come from the back of the restaurant and were setting up the camera to catch the show. Shawna looked nervous, something that was rare for her. Larry's pale face was absolutely white. He looked like he was about to be sick. Jim's stomach sank, and he felt like the room was about to start spinning, but Shawna found them standing there, made eye contact with him, and nodded her head. She smiled slightly. This one look made him feel better, but he wasn't sure they had any type of plan. Whatever the look meant, he was clinging to hope.

Everybody waited.

After about five minutes of suspense-filled waiting, the left door opened and one of the Mortons walked out. It was the older one. Jim hated the smug look on his wrinkled face. Just by his sneer, Jim could tell this was going to be horrible.

"Mornin', everyone! We have quite a special treat for y'all." He paused and drank in the attention, his beady eyes shining.

"We've all been well aware of what's been happenin' in these woods. Strange things seen, we've all heard stories. Now these TV folks show up and start askin' all sorts of questions and havin' some sort of, ah, encounter." He paused again as a murmur went through the crowd.

Jim heard a woman nearby say, "Scary, scary."

Not a good sign.

Mr. Morton continued. "What we have to show you is actually pretty terrifyin'. What we have is somethin' that ain't supposed to exist. It's somethin' that ain't talked about in the Bible."

The last part elicited quite a few gasps from the audience, mostly women. Jim started to feel panicked. He wanted to get up and shout, do something. He looked at his family, and they looked the same way—caged. Jack's eyes were bouncing from Mr. Morton, to the audience, to the back of the room, like he was trying to figure out an escape plan or something.

"My brother is going to bring in the *monsters*, yes, *monsters*," he paused here. "And yes, monsters, meaning more than one. When he does, I'll explain exactly what happened and how many we think there are around here, ready to terrorize us all."

Another dramatic pause and dramatic look around the room. Jim's panic was rising with each second, and he felt like he couldn't breathe. His knees were bouncing as he leaned against the wall. He felt like he had to move now. Could he create some kind of diversion? Would anybody be able to do anything? Would people let this go after all the build-up?

Mr. Morton opened his mouth to speak again, but a crashing sound came from the back. Mr. Morton's mouth snapped shut, and his eyes narrowed. He looked more confused than anybody else. His eyes suddenly widened, and he shot off the stage at a run.

Jim looked to his dad, who was staring ahead, just as confused as Jim was, then he looked to see if Shawna knew what was happening. That's when he noticed that she and Pete were both missing. Larry was manning the camera, which he never did.

Something was happening.

Looking at Jack, Jim saw that he had noticed the same thing. Involuntarily, he took a step to follow Mr. Morton. He noticed his dad did the same. With one look at Karen, they knew she and Jilly would split up and head for the Jeep, out of the way. They all moved at once, with Jim and Jack moving in unison toward the back of the diner, but Larry was waving frantically at them. Jim caught his eye, and Larry nodded his chin to the side door as he moved toward the front of the diner. Jack was ahead and immediately veered to the side. He and Jim both slipped out the door while Jim took one last look back. The room was beginning to turn to chaos. Mr. Morton was disappearing through the back door in hurry.

Jim let the door fall and turned to his dad. They were outside Mel's, in a small employee parking lot that was more like a small alleyway. Jim saw Shawna fly around the corner of the diner. She didn't slow as she passed them; she just yelled out, "Help Pete! Run to the van!"

A crash sounded from behind Mel's, and Pete was suddenly rounding the corner. He was a sight. If the situation wasn't so serious, Jim might have laughed. Pete had the baby in his awkward arms, and was being half choked by the boy. He was hanging on to Pete's neck, legs around his waist, swinging side to side, looking this way and that. Every few steps, he would drop down and run with Pete, then jump back onto Pete's back. He looked like a wild animal, eyes huge and practically spinning in his head.

"Dudes! Help me get them to the van!"

Jim jumped into gear and ran forward to grab the boy's hand. The boy's eyes were flitting around wildly, but as soon as Jim grabbed his hand and forearm firmly, his eyes lit on Jim's. His jerky movements smoothed out, and he started running in stride with Jim. Jack ran ahead and disappeared around the front corner of the building. Jim knew he was trying to tell Karen what was happening.

Apparently they had moved the van to the employee lot at some point, and Shawna was now inside and starting the engine. She backed it up and positioned it for a hasty exit, tires kicking up gravel. Pete and Jim rushed to the van and slammed opened the back door. Pete jumped in and carefully set the baby down, then turned to help Jim, who was struggling with the boy. As soon as the van door had opened, he had started pulling from Jim's grasp. Jim couldn't believe how strong he was. It was clear he was only using part of his strength, yet he was nearly throwing Jim off balance. Jim couldn't see how the Mortons had been able to take him.

"It's okay, it's okay. We're here to help," Jim tried to soothe him.

"We need to hurry," Pete said. "Come on, little dude. We'll take you to your parents."

The boy was breathing so hard and fast it looked like he might pass out. Jim felt so badly for him. His eyes were still wild and welling up with tears. His shoulders started to hunch, and he looked sad and vulnerable.

"Come on, son. We'll help you." Jack's voice was so soft but firm and confident. Jim looked at his dad with new respect at his ability to be so nice to the boy.

The boy looked at Jack and finally relented. They all piled into the van, and as soon as the door slammed shut, they were speeding off down the main road. Those in the back were bumping around, trying to keep upright. Jack had his strong arms around the baby, holding her safe and tight.

As they sped out of the drive and onto the main road, Jim saw their Jeep fall into line behind them. His mother was at the wheel and Larry was in the passenger seat. He had forgotten all about Larry! Jilly's little, pale face was barely visible in the back.

They flew down the road, and Shawna started making twists and turns that got Jim lost. Jack was barking out directions. Jim just stayed close to the boy and tried to keep reassuring him that everything would be okay. Knowing that he didn't understand his language, Jim tried to use facial expressions and body language, but he felt like he had no idea what he was doing. Still, the boy seemed to be calming down. Either that or he was shutting down and trying to be invisible. Jim hoped it wasn't that.

Looking out the back window, Jim saw that nobody was chasing them. *What?*

"Hey, nobody's following," he yelled to the front.

Shawna looked at him in the rear-view mirror. "Yeah, well, we took care of the Morton's cars. Their tires looked a little full, so we let some air out of them. With a knife."

Jim couldn't help but laugh.

They had made such a hasty exit, with plenty of turns thrown in, that nobody followed them all the way back to the farm.

The drive to the barn was quiet, which made Jim uneasy, but he was hopeful. There just hadn't been time for anyone to react. Nobody inside the diner had known what was happening, and it had only been the Mortons who were dealing with the bigfoot. Maybe they were in the clear.

Shawna skidded to a stop in front of the barn, and they opened the back door. The boy kept himself pressed into the corner until Jim stepped out and gestured for him to follow. He finally relaxed ever so slightly and unfolded his legs. Jim grabbed his arm for reassurance again, and led him out. The boy looked around for a moment, then his eyes widened. His back straightened, and he looked better.

The barn door burst open, and Scar and the mother covered the distance in an instant. Jim was stunned at how fast they were for their size. They enveloped both the boy and the baby in tight hugs and began inspecting each of them while uttering soft grunting and cooing sounds. Jim could feel their relief and joy.

Scar broke away from his family and moved toward Jack. He shifted a bit uncomfortably on his feet and then gave Jack a nod. The look in his eye couldn't be mistaken—he was beyond grateful. Jack gave him a nod back and smiled. Scar looked around at the group, and Jim knew that he was thanking them all for what they had done for his family.

Charlie suddenly appeared beside Jim. He picked Jim up in a tight squeeze and didn't let him go for a long time. Finally, he released him and gave the rest of the family the same famous hug. When he got to Shawna, she beamed up at him. Jim thought he might pat her on the shoulder, but he actually picked her up, too. He went right down the line and hugged Pete and Larry, as well, leaving each of them with stupidly huge grins on their faces.

They started describing his hug to each other, as if they hadn't experienced the same thing. "He's so hairy! Oh my God!"

"Did you feel his muscles? He's like a rock!"

"I felt like a little kid being hugged by some giant!"

Jim laughed at them. He felt so happy.

Jack's voice broke through the celebration. "We should get inside and figure out how to get everyone out of here. Fast."

Everyone silently sobered up, their faces again turning serious, and began moving inside. The bigfoot family looked at them and back to the woods. They were obviously wanting to leave and probably never see another human being again. Jim looked at Charlie, but Charlie was already moving toward the family. He seemed to have a small conversation with them and waved a thick arm for them to follow. Everyone went inside, including the reluctant bigfoot family.

Once inside, Jack began. "First, how did you get them?"

"That other Morton guy isn't the smartest," Pete said. "He made the mistake of turning his back, got shoved into a closet. Tragically, the door got wedged shut," he made a gasping sound, "and he couldn't get out, so we took the kids."

"Poor dumb Morton," Jim joked.

Shawna snorted, then said, "Jackasses had some drugs they were giving them. Must have been how they got the boy in the first place. Must have pounced when their parents were off gathering food or something. I don't know. Guess they didn't want them too drugged for their debut, though."

After a moment of the group digesting that sickening bit of information, Jack got down to business. "We need to leave here, but they need to leave here, too. They're not safe here. I know they would prefer to slip into the woods and never be seen again, but with these people out there, I just don't want to take that chance, even if it may be small. We can take them away from here and let them out wherever they want, but I just think we should take them away. It would be quicker for them if we help."

"I agree," Karen said. The others echoed her sentiment. Jilly yelled out a late, "I agree!"

After about a second of letting that sink in, everyone started moving at once. Shawna, Pete, and Larry had already moved out of the small bed and breakfast, so they began loading their van with the things they had left in the barn. Jack and Jim started getting the RV ready to go, while Karen talked to Charlie, trying to get him to understand what the plan was. He seemed to get it immediately, and Jim thought he already wanted to take the family away from there. That thought made Jim wonder what Charlie wanted with them, but he wouldn't worry about that now.

CHAPTER TWENTY-THREE
Time to Leave

EVERYONE WAS READY in minutes, and they got the Jeep hooked up for towing, faster than ever before. They decided to meet a little ways out of town. There was a place an hour away that Jim and his family had passed on their way there. It was a campground that offered remote cabins near a lake, and they had seen that hardly anyone was currently staying there. It would be the perfect spot for them to meet and regroup.

They needed a permanent plan for the new family.

Pete started up the van and began leading the way down the driveway. Jim noticed that the van was sitting lower than usual with the weight of the bigfoot family inside. He hoped it could handle their weight. Charlie was with his family in the RV, but he was keeping an eye on the van and his new friends.

Jack had planned for them to leave in a roundabout way, rather than down the main road again. It would take them longer, but hopefully they could avoid anyone who was looking for them. Pete turned away from the town and began the route to skirt the main part of town. They turned left onto a small dirt road that would lead them by another farm. Jim could see a long way off, and what he saw made him blink in surprise. Down the long road was what appeared to be a roadblock. A truck was parked sideways across the road, and another vehicle was behind it. There were four men standing behind the truck.

Jim saw Pete stop, and Jack did the same. There was only a slight pause before Jack started backing down the road. There was nowhere to turn around, so they had to back up. Jim was glad they hadn't traveled too far down the road, because Jack was going faster than he felt comfortable with. Jim noticed Karen was holding her breath.

They made it back to the main road, and Jack quickly sped off down the other way. Jim tried to keep eyes on the men, but they were getting too far away to see clearly. Still, he thought he saw the vehicles starting to leave before they were completely out of view.

Jack drove quickly down the road, the van following. He started mumbling directions, trying to navigate the unfamiliar routes. He took them back to the farm road and passed it. The first small dirt road they came upon, he took. It was almost not even a road. Jim wondered just where Jack was going, but his tense posture and narrowed eyes told Jim he was concentrating hard. They took a left, then a right, and another left in a zigzag pattern that made Jilly say that it felt like a theme park ride. Jim looked at her, sitting across from him on the couch, but she wasn't having fun; she was looking rather serious. Her little brows were scrunched together. She was trying to watch the road, but she was so small that it was hard for her to see around and over the two front seats.

A quick turn jolted Jim's attention back to the road. They had almost missed a nearly invisible turn that was hidden among a huge crowd of trees. Jim could now clearly see a larger road ahead. They were making it out of this small, wooded maze.

The road ahead had a sign indicating that the next town was to the right, so they turned that way. After several minutes, Jim felt himself relaxing. He realized his legs had been very tense, and the muscles were now loosening.

"Oh no," Karen said.

Jim looked up to see another roadblock. It was another set of trucks with about five men moving around. A chill of fear went through Jim's body. This was not good. They weren't letting them out. He looked at Charlie, whose eyes were wide. He understood that they were in trouble.

Jim's phone rang. It was Shawna.

"Yeah?"

"Is that what I think it is?"

"Yep. Another roadblock. What are we doing, Dad?" He could hear Shawna confirming to Pete and Larry that it was a roadblock, and he heard a cursed reply from Pete.

"I don't know, but we can't go this way." He turned abruptly at a small road to the left. Jim could see the men moving to get back in their trucks, but the thick trees they disappeared into blocked him from seeing what they did next.

"This is unbelievable!" Shawna cried into the phone. She sounded hysterical but mad. "Who are these people?"

Jim lost track of where they were. "Do you know where we're going, Dad?"

"Right now, back to where we started."

"Go to the main road. Through town," Karen said.

"What?" Jack asked.

Jim thought that would be the same as giving up.

"They're obviously covering the more secret ways out of here, but will they be able to do that in the middle of the busy town? Can they actually block us in front of the entire town?"

A voice squeaked from Jim's hand. He put the phone back to his ear and heard Shawna. "She's right! Let's go there. That's the best chance we have."

"Shawna agrees," Jim said.

Jack turned onto the main road. "All right. Let's try this," he said.

They rode in tense silence. The air felt like it was buzzing with their anxious energy. Jim looked at Charlie again and saw that he was staring at the van, out the back window. He turned back around and gave Jim a feeble smile. His worry about the others was obvious.

The drive felt both unbearably long and unnervingly short, all at the same time. The tops of buildings began to appear on the horizon and quickly grew into a full-fledged town. Jim saw that it was just as crowded as when they left, with trucks and people moving all about. They slowed and drove through Bisby, headed to the diner—smack dab in the middle of town.

Jim saw that people began noticing them. People were stopping and staring. He hoped that somehow this would all stop and they would be able to get out of here.

No such luck.

As soon as he thought they might be able to get out, he saw the Mortons take to the street. They had been stationed at Mel's and apparently had been told of the newcomer's arrival. Each of them had smug sneers on their faces and fire in their eyes.

Jack started to drive by, but a sheriff's car drove up quickly and blocked them. The old sheriff got out and stood, waiting. Jim hadn't seen him before, but he would have definitely guessed this man was the sheriff. He just looked like a sheriff. The sheriff was a big man who had gone soft with age, but he would still intimidate most people. His skin was worn from years of being outside, and his eyes had a steely glint to them.

"Guess we have to stop," Jack said. He blew out a long breath and looked back at his family.

CHAPTER TWENTY-FOUR
Running Scared

THIS WAS IT.

They were going to be stopped and found out. Charlie and the bigfoot family would be found, everyone would see them, and it would be over. Their lives as they knew them were over. Charlie knew what was happening and moved quickly and stealthily to the back of the RV, out of sight.

Jim felt like he was in a dream. A bad dream. They were never going to recover from this. He felt like everything was happening in slow motion as the sheriff walked up to Jack's window. He noticed that the sheriff's deputy was walking around the other side of the RV and back toward the van. The deputy stopped in front of the passenger side window of the van, with his hand on his gun, ready.

Jack rolled down the window, and the sheriff stopped there.

"Hello there. Now the Mortons there say you stole something extremely valuable from them. If that's true, you're going to have to answer for that." As he talked, Jim noticed his eyes were roaming all over everything he could see inside the RV. Jilly waved at him. To Jim's surprise, he saw the man's mouth twitch slightly at her gesture, but he kept a ready stance.

"No, sir. We stole nothing of theirs," Jack answered.

That was true. The boy and baby weren't theirs. And technically Pete and Shawna stole them. Well, Jim and his family did help.

"Well, would you mind if I have a look inside there? We need to talk to your friends, too," he said, nodding in the direction of the van.

"Actually, I do. I have my family in here, my children. We didn't take anything of theirs, and this feels like harassment."

The sheriff shifted uncomfortably. "Now hold your horses. I had to ask because the Mortons have claimed that you stole something from them. If we can settle this in a civil manner, that would be best."

"Sheriff! Sheriff, what are you waitin' for?" one of the Mortons hollered. It was the older one who had been talking at Mel's. Jim hated his beady eyes.

"Hold up, Chick. We're talking here."

Chick?

"I ain't holdin' up. They stole our stuff. It's either in there or in the van."

"Chick, let me handle it." The sheriff suddenly went from a nice, mild-mannered country gentleman to a no-nonsense lawman. His whole demeanor changed, and Jim was impressed.

Chick Morton scoffed at the sheriff's lack of support, and stood there huffing on the sidewalk. The other Morton joined him, and they watched the rest of the scene quietly from there.

The sheriff turned his attention back to Jack. "Sir, will you consent to a search of your motor coach?"

"I'm sorry, but we didn't take anything, and I won't let you search based on their wild claims." Jim could see a trickle of sweat run down this side of his dad's forehead.

The sheriff started to say something, but he was cut off by Mr. Walker.

"Sheriff Barlow, what seems to be the problem here?" Mr. Walker was strolling across the street from Mel's. He had a pleasant smile plastered on his face, but Jim could see his eyes were tense.

"Dale, this doesn't really concern you. I appreciate the concern, though."

"Well, Sheriff, I heard that these people are being accused of stealing from the Mortons there. I know they didn't take anything from the Mortons. If it's a matter of word, I hope that mine carries at least some weight."

Sheriff Barlow took a breath, and his tension visibly dissolved. He walked a few paces away, toward Mr. Walker, but Jim could still hear them.

"Well, Dale, I'm glad you came over and gave me your take. I know the Mortons can get worked up over nothing, so I'm glad to have someone of your standing give their opinion." He glanced back at Jack. "And it don't help that the brothers won't say what they supposedly took."

"I can say that the family there went outside and went right to their vehicle. Far as I know, they left right after that. Then I hear about some roadblocks and stuff happening, and I know you didn't have anything to do with that."

At that, Sheriff Barlow stiffened. "No, sir. I sure didn't authorize any roadblocks." He let out a piercing whistle. "Chick, get over here. You too, Clint."

Chick and Clint exchanged confused glances that made Jim think of when kids are in trouble and look to each other for help. Chick began walking up with a scowl on his face. Clint followed behind, subconsciously distancing himself from the trouble.

"Sheriff, aren't you going to arrest them?" Chick's beady eyes flicked nervously up at Jack, as he licked his lizard lips.

"What am I hearing about roadblocks?" Sheriff Barlow's eyes were zeroed in on Chick, who looked like he had been struck. He quickly recovered enough to speak, but he sputtered.

"Sheriff, we were about to show everyone somethin' real valuable, and those people took it. So yes, we had some of our people put up near the back ways out of town to make sure they didn't get away with our property." He stuck out his chin and planted his hands on his narrow hips.

"Calm down now. Mr. Walker here says that nothing happened. He's a very upstanding man in town here, so I have to take his word, too. I can't just go around searching folks' cars based on this. These folks are from out of town, and that's not how we treat guests."

"I don't care about tourists, I care about my money! They stole something that could make us rich. If you won't—"

A banging sound cut Chick off mid-threat. It was coming from the van.

Jim's stomach sank. Something was happening with the family. He heard Shawna shout. Standing up to look out the back window, he could see Pete jump out of the van, leaving the door flung open, and run toward the back. Jim flew through the RV door and ran to the van.

Shawna and Pete were standing around the back of the van.

"Hey, man! You can't do that!" Pete said.

Clint Morton was standing near the back doors of the van, breathing hard. He had a bat in his hand and had obviously been trying to break into the van. Sheriff Barlow's deputy was poised, gun drawn, and trying to talk him down.

"Sir, you're going to have to stop that and sit down over there on the curb."

Clint looked frenzied, his eyes big and wild, but he visibly calmed and moved to the curb.

"What in—"

Sheriff Barlow's question was cut off as the van's door burst open and a brown, hairy wall shot past the crowd. Traffic in the cross street stopped Scar and the mother, who were each carrying a child, and they paused to look around for an escape route.

The fear Jim felt was paralyzing. He looked at Sheriff Barlow, whose jaw was slack with amazement. In fact, everyone in the vicinity had similar looks of shock on their faces. Almost comically, Jim noticed the man who had sent them to Bisby, the man from the wildlife park. He was in the same khaki outfit he had been wearing when they had met him, standing there on the curb, mouth hanging open.

This was bad.

Jim felt someone grab his shoulder. Looking up, he saw Jack trying to pull him back to the RV, and then he finally felt like he could move. They ran to the RV, and Jim tried to see just how many people were able to see this.

Too many.

As he ran, he heard Shawna and Pete slam the doors to the van and start it up. He jumped into the RV, where Karen was struggling with Charlie. He looked terrified. His eyes were glued to the family still moving about in the center of town, as he was trying to get past Karen to the door, but only halfheartedly. He knew the risks and that the smart thing was to stay there.

"Charlie! It'll be okay," Jim said. "We'll get them."

Charlie looked down at him and slowly sat on the floor of the RV. Everyone barely had time to get seated before Jack lurched the RV forward. The bulky vehicle wasn't easy to maneuver quickly, but Jack was doing a good job. They edged around trucks that had slowed or completely stopped to witness the spectacle unfolding on the typically quiet streets of Bisby.

Jim was struck by how quickly the bigfoot family was able to move through the town. They were quick for their size, and they obviously had a massive adrenalin surge, but they were still having trouble navigating through the busy streets. The weekend had brought out many people, and the Mortons' promise of something exciting had gathered everyone in the heart of Bisby. Scar and his family were trying to avoid people and vehicles and were instinctively making turns down less-crowded streets. It would have been faster to keep on a straight line out of the town, but they were moving forward a block, then over a block, and losing time.

It was beyond frustrating for Jim. He couldn't believe this. The secret was out.

Jack was trying his best to move along with the bigfoot family, but they were lagging behind. Scar started to lead his family across the street, obviously aiming for a quiet alleyway that would take them another block down. Just then, a group of high school kids in a large truck came to a screeching halt right in front of the family, just missing them. Seeing that the family was okay, Jim took a breath and realized that he had been holding it.

Jack had finally had enough.

"Karen, you take over. We'll be in contact through phone, but we're going out there on foot. It'll be quicker that way."

She nodded, and Jack pulled over quickly. He and Jim jumped out of the RV and began pursuit on foot.

Just then, a siren wailed.

The sheriff was joining the chase and coming up fast from behind. Karen pulled out to make her way out of town at the exact moment that the sheriff was trying to pass her. As they ran, Jim heard her yell a loud, "Sorry!"

Way to go, Mom.

Jack and Jim moved quickly to the still-frozen family. Scar was still standing in front of his family, breathing hard, while the high school kids sat staring, mouths gaping. Jim was surprised that none of them had begun snapping pictures with their cell phones yet. Just as he thought that, he heard one of them yell, "What the hell is that? Someone get a picture!"

Not waiting to give them a good shot, Jim and Jack reached the family and pulled them into the alley. Jim didn't think they had time to get their cameras handy, but either way, what was done was done. At this point, Scar and his family gave in to Jim and Jack. They were letting them lead and trusting them to get them to safety. The alley wasn't deep, and they carefully exited beside some less populated stores. This part of town was quiet—the excitement hadn't yet reached the outskirts.

Breathing hard, Jim looked back and saw the truck pulling even with the alley for a better look. Jim pushed the family in front of the store, out of view. The store, it turned out, was a book store, with a display of some children's book in the front window. Jim almost laughed at the ape on the cover. *Of course.* Peering inside, Jim couldn't see anyone, but a door was open in the back, and a light was shining out. Someone was in there, but they were busy in the back.

Lucky for us.

"Jim, we need to hurry. We'll go across here and down that alley over there, but we'll be exposed. We need to make it over to the RV park. Tell your mom."

Jim nodded. He was turned around, but now that Jack said it, he realized that the RV park was nearby. If they could keep moving down the side streets, they could cut over and be near the wooded area behind the park. As they ran, he pulled out his phone and dialed his mom. She would make her way to the park and wait for them there. "Tell Shawna!" he said and ended the call.

The group moved into a large doorway of a small pizza shop that had apparently closed. It was probably like the pizza shop in a small town near where Jim and his family lived. That one was always closing up and being re-opened by another sentimental resident. Whatever the case with this one, nobody was inside, so they had a bit of a reprieve.

They had crossed the street without drawing any attention. It helped that nobody was out and about on this street, except for an old man in suspenders who had walked into a shop a couple blocks down. He hadn't looked around.

The sound of a rumbling truck brought Jim's attention to the right. The group peeked out of their hiding place and saw a beat-up, tan and white Ford idling in the cross-section of the street. They all pulled their heads back quickly and stayed quiet. After a minute, the truck moved on.

They were on the hunt.

Jim felt lucky that nobody else was driving around. Just as he thought that, a line of trucks appeared. They were turning down their street, and all were blaring horns and yelling about the game. Chants of "let's go Bluejays!" were being screamed as they drove along. They were approaching fast, so the hiding group really had nowhere to go. The best they could do was to sit still and hope those in the vehicles didn't notice them as they passed in their excitement.

They were a few yards away when one of the trucks backfired. Scar shot out like a spooked horse, dragging his family with him. Jim and Jack had no time to react. They were just too fast. The first truck was slow to react, but a screech told Jim that they had seen it. He heard the screech of other brakes as the trucks behind the first slammed to a stop to avoid hitting the ones in front.

Jim didn't wait to see if there was a crash; he just took off after the family.

This was going to be bad.

It was amazing how quick they were. Those long, powerful legs really propelled them forward, and Jim felt like he could never keep up.

"Stop!" he yelled. "Stop, it's okay! We'll help you!"

They didn't seem to hear; they were deaf with fear. Either that or they didn't trust him anymore.

Scar kept going and turned left down a side street. Jim and Jack were pumping their legs as quickly as they could to keep up. Jim was afraid they would disappear around the corner, but apparently they had slowed to get their bearings or figure out where to go, because when he and Jack turned the corner, they could see them rounding the next corner to the right.

"Oh no," Jack huffed out.

"What?"

"They're heading for the baseball field."

"Oh great. But they'll avoid the crowd for sure, right?," Jim yelled. He realized his strained running was causing him to yell.

"Yeah, I hope so."

They kept going, not running into anyone else as they went. Jim couldn't figure out why nobody was over here. When they took another left, he realized why. They were coming into the back of the baseball field, where nobody was because everyone was in the stadium. Being a Texas town, baseball was huge here—maybe not as big as football—and most people were in the stadium, ready to cheer their team to the win.

It was strangely quiet in the stadium. Jim couldn't figure out why.

The stadium was situated near the edge of town but not quite. The school was next to it, along with the junior high and elementary schools. Around those were other buildings; beyond those were the woods.

He looked up and saw Scar and the family heading for the corner of the stadium that opened up to the back corner of the field. From here, he could see grass, which is probably what attracted the family to it. They had no idea they were heading *into the stadium.*

Jack and Jim started shouting to get their attention, but the family made no indication that they heard them. They watched helplessly as the family ran straight into the opening. This danger

gave Jim enough energy to pick up his pace, but it was still agoniz-
ingly slow.

    Finally, Jack and Jim burst into the stadium. What they saw,
Jim would never forget.

CHAPTER TWENTY-FIVE
Found

THE STADIUM WAS still bizarrely quiet except for some gasps and murmurs. Standing in the outfield was the bigfoot family. The were huddled together, spinning slowly to take in their surroundings. The players were lined up, each team along one baseline, but those toward the outfield were moving toward the infield and looked confused.

Looking in the stands, Jim saw signs for both teams, but also more prominently at the moment, signs that said, "We will never forget," and "We miss you, Dan." It finally dawned on Jim that they had interrupted a moment of silence.

Seconds ticked by, with just a quiet buzzing, then the whole place erupted. Jim wasn't prepared for the noise, and neither was the bigfoot family, who ducked and began running in circles like a dog trying to get away from a scary noise.

Jim ran forward and grabbed Scar's arm, and Jack grabbed the other. They began leading them away from the field, back the way they had come. People were yelling, some were running forward. There was a security officer slowly making his way to them, but to Jim's surprise, he was laughing. In fact, Jim looked around to see many smiling, laughing faces. He heard a guy on the sideline yell out, "Nice try, Mustangs!" Another one yelled, "Is that the new Bisby Monster mascot?" There were a few who had serious faces, and a child was crying.

Before Jim could take in any more reactions, they were to the opening of the field. There was a group of people converging on the spot, and Jack tried to hurry Scar and his family away, but they caught them. When they were a few feet away, Jack jumped out in front of them to head them off while motioning to Jim to get the family away.

"Hey, man! Those are awesome costumes. Where did you get them?"

"Who are you guys?"

"You with Lakeville?"

Jim didn't stick around to see what Jack was saying. He just kept pushing them out, then began leading them through the back of the parking lot and around the neighboring library building. The woods were only feet away, but Jack was still gone. Jim went ahead and plunged into the woods, taking the family far inside the safety of the greenery. He stopped behind a stand of trees and peeked around it. From here, he could look out for Jack, but he also saw a small group of people standing next to the library and looking in his direction.

They had seen them flee.

After a few minutes, Jack came pushing through the small group that was still standing there talking about what they had just seen. He ran around the back of the library and then into the woods to Jim's right. He kept going straight back, so Jim called out to him, softly.

His head snapped in the direction of Jim's call, and he started making his way over. Finally spotting them, he hurried over. The group was together again.

Now they just had to get to Karen and Jilly and get out of here.

CHAPTER TWENTY-SIX
Savior

JACK STEPPED OUT and looked up and down the street. "Let's go."

The group moved forward again, with Jack in the lead and Jim bringing up the rear. Jim was watching the family. The boy was hunched over with fear. He kept grabbing Scar's arm or hand for comfort and holding on for a few seconds, then letting go. The mother was standing taller. She had the fierce look of a mother who wasn't going to let anything happen to her babies.

And Jim believed it.

It was eerie. Jim could hear engines coming and going all around them. He heard people yelling, talking. It all was the noise of people hunting for them.

They made their way slowly to the edge of the commercial tract of town. Across the next street was the wooded lot that backed up to the RV park. They paused behind a dumpster and watched for a moment. Nobody was moving in this area. Down the street, a stray dog with matted hair was nosing around some trash on the shoulder of the road. It raised its head and sniffed the air, then turned to look in their direction. Another sniff, and it turned and ran away.

Jim had the paranoid feeling that it was going to tell someone where they were, like Lassie. He snorted at himself. The boy looked at him, his eyes telling Jim he was curious about why Jim snorted.

"Okay, we're clear," Jack said. They stood and ran for the trees.

Just as they plunged into the welcoming embrace of the thick woods, Jim heard another loud engine close in on them. He quickened his pace, and they all ducked down, even though the trees, brush, and vines were so thick that anyone would have a difficult time seeing them.

The group looked at each other. Jim felt their hesitance to feel even slightly safe here, but the truth was they did. The woods were home. He could see the lessening of fear in their eyes. Slowly, they all stood and began walking. The family stayed in a tight formation, with Jack and Jim in the lead. They could still hear the loud sounds of the town. It was creepy knowing they were out there searching for them.

Ahead, Jim heard a twig break and he froze. They all froze. Nothing was there. Jim was straining his eyes to see something, anything. Finally, Charlie stepped forward.

"Charlie!" Jim rushed forward to greet him. He wrapped Jim up in a massive hug, then moved to Jack and the family.

"You shouldn't be out here," Jack said. "Let's go."

Charlie led the way back at a brisk pace. Jim texted his mom and Shawna, letting them know where they were and that Charlie was with them. Karen was relieved, since Charlie had run off without them as soon as they had stopped.

Before long, they were at the edge of the trees, looking into the RV park. Everything looked quiet. Karen had backed into a spot near where they had stayed before. She had chosen the spot well. From there, they could pull straight out and speed away, hopefully forever. The van was next to it, engine idling. Shawna, Pete, and Larry were outside, looking anxious. They were pacing and talking quietly.

"Come on," Jack said with a wave.

They started to break through the trees, when a truck came speeding up the driveway of the park.

Jack put his arms out and ushered them back into hiding. They watched the truck pull right up to their RV and the van. Jim was holding his breath but let it out when Mr. Walker and Eva got out of the truck. The two newcomers ran to meet the group at the van and RV.

Jim looked at his dad, who looked at Charlie and said, "Stay here." Jack and Jim left the cover of the woods and met the small group. As they got closer, Jim heard Mr. Walker say, "They'll be here in a matter of minutes."

"Who?" Jack asked.

Mr. Walker and Eva turned to see them approach. Eva's eyes grew big at the sight of Jim, and she blushed. Karen and Jilly hugged both of them. Shawna, Pete, and Larry all gave them a round of smiles and greetings. "Good to see ya," Shawna finished.

"The Mortons, Sheriff Barlow. You name it, they're coming," Mr. Walker answered Jacks question.

Jim's stomach tightened again. They were so close. Couldn't they just leave them alone?

Jack winced. "Great. We're sitting ducks here."

"We'd like to help," Eva said. Her voice was soft but determined. She looked at Jim with fiery eyes, and he couldn't help but smile. Embarrassed, he looked around. Pete gave him a wink that made him blush.

"So then you know what we're doing here," Shawna said.

"We do," Mr. Walker replied. "You have a family of bigfoot, bigfoots? Bigfeet? Whatever. And you're trying to save them. We'd like to help. They saved Eva here." He put his arm around his daughter.

"Okay, so all secrets aside, we do have them, and we're trying to take them far away from here, where they'll be safe," Jack said. "But they're looking for our RV and their van, so we can't take them out with those."

Everyone turned to look at Mr. Walker's truck. Unlike most in town, it was shiny and new. Amazingly, it actually had one of those hard covers for the bed that made it look like an SUV. Nobody else had one because they typically used the bed for hauling things. Mr. Walker was more of a genteel man who didn't have much use for hauling large things, Jim guessed.

Mr. Walker looked back at Jack and said, "Use my truck. If they can fit," he added.

It would be a squeeze. After all, these creatures were huge.

"Let's try it," Pete said.

Jim turned and called for Charlie.

"They have names?" Eva asked.

"Well, mine does," Jim answered.

She blinked, and then her eyes popped out. "Yours? What do you mean?"

"Well, we found one living in our woods last year. His name is Charlie. Now these, we haven't named them yet. Been too busy."

"You've got to be kidding me. This is amazing!" She laughed a high, pretty sound and clapped her hands like a little girl.

Jilly was watching and automatically clapped along with her. "I love Charlie," she told Eva.

Eva smiled at her and turned to the woods just as Charlie was emerging, the family closely behind him.

Her smile grew and then her mouth dropped open.

"This is the best thing I've ever seen."

Charlie loped up to Jim and looked ready for action. His usual laid back attitude was replaced with that of a soldier ready to move.

"Charlie!" Jilly caught sight of him, squealed and reached up for him to pick her up. He swung her up and hugged her tightly.

"Charlie, this is Eva. She and her dad are going to help us. Eva, this is Charlie, my best friend."

She put out her hand, and he grabbed it gently. She giggled and said, "Nice to meet you." Charlie smiled back at her.

"So you lied to me, then?" Eva asked Jim. Her eyes were sparkling, and he could tell she wasn't really mad.

"Sorry, but I didn't know if I should tell you. Sorry." He was still nervous about having lied to her.

Eva laughed. "It's okay! I would have lied if I were you. Can't be too careful with something like this."

Scar and his family moved close but wouldn't stand more than a few feet away from the newcomers. They were understandably less trusting right now.

Jim nudged Charlie and pointed back at Scar and the others. Charlie immediately went over and began communicating with the scared family. Jim was sad to see the fear in their eyes and wanted to be able to get them to safety.

He walked to the truck, where Jack and Mr. Walker were talking. Pete and Larry were moving some boxes out of the truck and into the van.

"What's the plan?" he asked.

Jack stopped talking to answer his question. "The Walkers are going to drive them out of here and to their house. We'll meet them there as soon as we can."

He looked around nervously. He hadn't said what they would have to deal with when the sheriff and the Mortons came, but he probably was trying to be optimistic.

"They'll be squeezed in tight, but I think they should be okay for a short ride." He paused and looked hard at Jim. "Jim, Charlie has to go with them. He can stay low in the back seat, but the others are going in the bed."

"I know. That's the only way to get him out, too." He stood up straight and tried to look more confident than he felt.

"Hey, Charlie! How ya doin', my man?" Pete said. Charlie had walked up, ready to move. The family had moved as one unit behind Charlie. They were staying close to him. Charlie greeted Pete, and Larry stuck out his hand very formally, but he actually gave Charlie a warm smile. Larry was loosening up.

There was a growling sound behind them that almost didn't register to Jim. He was too focused on engine sounds and other human noises. He looked back and saw that matted dog standing there growling at the strange creatures before it. Its hackles were raised, and its yellowed teeth were bared.

The boy broke away from Scar and strode confidently up to the dog. He reached out his hand and began petting it. Jim couldn't believe it. He looked so strange, standing there with all his hair and petting the dog like any other boy might do. The dog visibly relaxed and actually wagged its scraggly tail.

"Gotta hurry, here," Mr. Walker said, breaking the momentary hold the spectacle had on them all.

Everyone began moving.

Jack helped Charlie show the family how to get inside the truck. It was a struggle at first. They were scared, their eyes wild, but Charlie showed them and they reluctantly followed his example. They took up every bit of space in that truck, and the bed was riding significantly lower than before they were inside.

Charlie had to squeeze in the back seat of the four-door truck. It was going to be a tight fit. Eva pushed her seat forward, but Charlie's eyes still narrowed in a wince. Before they closed the door, Jim leaned in to say goodbye to Charlie.

"You take care of them and be safe, Charlie. We'll be back for you."

Charlie smiled at him with that toothy, chimp smile that he had sometimes, and Jim shut the door. Mr. Walker got in the truck, and Eva looked at Jim. She smiled before they took off. The

Walkers drove down the driveway and out of sight. Jim finally felt like a huge weight had been lifted from his shoulders.

They were safe.

No sooner had they gone than they began to hear other engines bearing down on their location.

They all stood there, waiting for the inevitable.

Jack looked around. "The truth. We didn't take anything of theirs. We were helping the family. Nothing about Charlie."

Curt nods answered him.

They didn't have to wait long.

CHAPTER TWENTY-SEVEN
Face the Music

SHERIFF BARLOW'S CAR was first, followed by a deputy's cruiser. The Mortons came next, followed by a couple of other trucks.

Sheriff Barlow pulled up directly in front of the group. He swung his heavy frame out and stood. He tipped his cowboy hat and sighed. "You people are hard to keep track of."

Jack played it cool. "Sorry, Sheriff. We were trying to get out of the way of the commotion."

Chick Morton jumped from his beat-up old truck and started yelling, "Sheriff! Sheriff, you need to arrest them. They're wreakin' havoc!"

Sheriff Barlow winced as Morton spoke, then turned to Jack and smiled slightly. "Now, I think y'all caused this commotion. You're going to need to come talk to me."

Pete cleared his throat. "Uh, who?"

"All of y'all. Are we going to have any problems?"

"No, sir," Jack said.

Sheriff Barlow's three deputies split up the family. Karen, Jim, and Jilly were kept together, Jack and Larry were put together, and Pete and Shawna were being interviewed by the sheriff.

The words weren't carrying, so Jim had no idea what was being said. Jilly was stuck to Karen's leg. She was scared. And it was understandable. A little kid sees a sheriff and knows their family is doing some secret stuff, they're going to think they're all going to jail. He grabbed her shoulder and gave it a squeeze. She turned her round, hazel eyes on him and he smiled.

"All right, you two stay over here," Sheriff Barlow said. He was walking over to Jack and Larry. They were next on the interrogation list.

Jim couldn't hear anything, and it was killing him. He had no idea what was being said by either side. Were they in terrible trouble? What was Jack telling him that they were doing? What did Shawna say? He looked at the Mortons, who were quietly fuming beside their truck. At least they weren't following the Walkers.

The last thought took Jim's mind to the Walkers and what they were doing with Charlie and the family. All he wanted to do was go get them and get out of here.

"Okay, let's see what these folks have to say," Sheriff Barlow said. Jim's head jerked toward the approaching sheriff. His palms were getting sweaty.

Karen stood in front of her children.

"Hello, ma'am. I'd like to talk to y'all a bit, but nothing too formal here." He peeked around her at Jilly and Jim. "Hi there, kids. How are y'all?"

"Fine," Jim replied coolly. Jilly was too scared to talk.

"Mind telling me what happened today?"

Karen took a breath. "We didn't take anything that belonged to them," she raised her chin in the direction of the Mortons.

"Okay, so what are we talking about here?"

She paused. Jim knew she was having trouble deciding how to answer. It was a difficult situation. How would the sheriff view it?

"You saw them."

He looked at her for a long moment, right in the eyes. Something about his eyes were soft and gentle, but there was a toughness that could possibly turn steely when necessary. Right now, they were soft and inquisitive.

"That I did. They're what I think they are?"

"They are." She was standing her ground confidently.

He took a deep breath and let it out slowly. "Okay. So you were trying to help them." It wasn't a question. He looked at Jim. "Son, if your mom here doesn't mind," he looked at Karen, who nodded., "I'd like to ask, is that what you saw in the woods? I heard about your story."

"Yes."

"And you found out there was a family?"

"Yes."

"And the Mortons came and took them?"

"They took the little ones."

"I see. And that's what they were, ah, unveiling at Mel's?"

"Yes."

"So you took them?"

"My family and I didn't. Not exactly. But we were helping them get to safety."

"Okay."

He looked at Jim for a moment longer, then turned around. "All right, guys, you three come here," he directed his deputies. They huddled together, with the sheriff talking, the deputies listening. Finally, Sheriff Barlow turned to the groups.

"Okay, folks, we have a unique situation here. We all saw the impossible today, and I think we can all agree that something like that … it ain't ever been seen before. So I can't say that something like that belongs to anybody. We can put two and two together. This TV gang has been out here looking at things, then this family here had some sort of encounter, then all of a sudden, the Mortons have something to show everyone. I think the events are connected. What I saw today, I can't say what they were, but I also can't say there's anything I can do for you, Chick and Clint."

"Sheriff! This ain't right." Chick Morton was fuming. He strode up to the sheriff, his beady eyes blazing. "They stole our property. We caught them; they were ours. It's not like they're *people*."

"I don't know what they are, but that's for someone smarter than me to decide. I can't go around giving you the rights to these things if they might end up on the protected list."

"Where are they now, Sheriff? Do they have them?" Chick asked.

"Well, that's a good question." Sheriff Barlow looked to Jack. "Where are they?"

Jack was about to answer, when barking stole everyone's attention. The matted dog had returned and was barking wildly into the woods. Jim was wondering just what the dog was barking at, when Chick Morton yelled, "They're in there! Let's go!"

The Mortons and their buddies ran past the group and into the woods. Sheriff Barlow and his deputies stayed where they were. The sheriff coughed, then turned to Jack and his family.

"These things caused quite a ruckus today, so I owed it to my town to hear you out about them. But since they haven't hurt anyone, I don't see any reason to launch a large man-hunt, so to speak."

He turned to his deputies. "You stay here and make sure the Mortons don't cause too much trouble. Don't let them run around with guns."

He turned back to Jim and his family and the TV crew. "Y'all should get moving along now." Then he turned around and walked with the sort of casual stride that only comes with living life in the country.

"So that was close," Shawna said.

"Lucky for us, the sheriff doesn't want trouble," Karen said.

"How about we not stick around too long?" Jim suggested.

"I like the way he thinks," Pete agreed, and all at once, they began moving for their vehicles. Nobody wanted to push their luck.

Jim climbed into the RV after Karen and Jilly and locked the door. He couldn't wait to get out of there and check on Charlie and the others. Everyone seemed to be moving too slowly, though.

He was anxious.

CHAPTER TWENTY-EIGHT
Escape

FINALLY, THEY WERE moving. Jack led the way out of the RV park, with Jim holding his breath, hoping that nobody else stopped them. They turned the same way the Walkers had when they had left earlier. Jack had Karen help him navigate the instructions Mr. Walker had left them. They were taken to the outskirts of town, where the woods were thick, but Jim found them inviting. Along the road, the greenery was so dense that anything could be lurking behind the first few feet, but nobody would be able to see it. Places like this always made Jim want to get in there and explore, but right now he was preoccupied.

"You think Charlie's okay?" he asked nobody in particular.

"Of course he is, honey," Karen answered. She was such a mom.

Jim looked at Jilly, who was sitting in the single chair behind Karen. She looked tiny in the cushioned seat, and Jim noticed that she was oddly quiet, which made her seem smaller. This was frightening to her.

"It'll be okay, Jilly. Don't worry. We're almost done."

She looked up at him and seemed confused. "I miss Banjo."

Jim wanted to laugh. She was in the middle of such a crazy, serious situation and she was missing the dog!

"He's okay. We'll see him soon enough."

She grinned up at him and looked happier after that.

The roads were set up in a sort of grid pattern, apparently around certain squares of farms. They kept making sharp turns, left and right, only seeming to go deeper into the Texas woods. Finally, they came to the end of the road, where a beautiful, wrought iron driveway gate stood. The road ended, and a pretty topped driveway began, leading the way farther into the green maze.

They sat before the gate that appeared locked. There was a solar panel that allowed for remote opening and closing, and a big Texas star emblazoned on the center of the gate itself. A keypad sat to the left. Jack opened his door and got out spryly. He punched in a code and the gate began to lazily swing open. He hopped back in, and they started slowly down the drive.

The path opened up immensely to reveal a sprawling piece of land situated in the middle of the deep Texas woods. Green grass that was well maintained created an inviting, civilized atmosphere that was in stark contrast to the wild woods around them.

"Okay, these people aren't the typical Bisby folks, are they?" Karen commented.

"Certainly not. And they have to have money to have created this," Jack replied.

Jim looked at the house. It was a beautiful two-story home that reminded him of a ranch house at a luxury resort and spa. It was as though it wasn't actually a working ranch house, it was only made to look like one. He saw that it had a wrap-around porch and stone that ran halfway up the walls. Outside, they had dug a small pond that had cattails, a pier, and a cabana. They had gone all out.

"This is crazy. This isn't like any other house here. At least I don't think," Jim said. Granted, they hadn't seen all of the homes in the town, and many were deep in the woods, too. But still, nothing they had seen so far was like this. He couldn't help but wonder about Mr. Walker.

Jim's phone rang. It was Shawna. "Are you seeing this? This house belongs in some upscale neighborhood, where people say stuff like, 'Muffy just won the state tennis tournament.'" Jim laughed and hung up.

They drove forward to where the limestone topped driveway became an expansive cement parking area in front of the garage, and then pulled in beside Mr. Walker's truck. Pete pulled up beside them.

Jack looked around. "Let's go."

They rushed out, Jim faster than the others. He was anxious about Charlie. A sound at the house alerted them to Mr. Walker's presence. He was coming out a side door that led to the large garage in front of them.

"There you are! That was faster than I thought it would be. Sheriff Barlow must not have wanted any trouble." He strode forward and shook all the men's hands, Jim's included; he gave polite nods to the ladies.

"He certainly didn't want any trouble. The Mortons are chasing phantoms in the woods behind the RV park," Jack answered. "Nice place you got here."

Jim heard a lot of agreeing murmurs.

"Thanks, thanks. Gracie and I really worked hard to get our dream home just right." He looked around and seemed to sense the unasked questions. "You're wondering what we're doing here?"

"It had crossed our minds," Jack answered. Everyone laughed a little.

"Well, I was born here but went to college and met Gracie. We both went to law school, became lawyers. We really lived quite a life together for years. Work was our lives. When Eva came along, Gracie quit, and we started looking at where we should settle. We thought it was important for Eva to know this part of life, too. So, we spend our summers and holidays here."

"So you're loaded," Pete said with his usual tact.

Mr. Walker let out a loud guffaw. "Now, son, I wouldn't say loaded, but we sure are comfortable." He winked. "Come on inside. I can tell this one is anxious to see his friend," he said, jabbing a thumb at Jim.

Karen grabbed Jilly's hand. "We'll wait out here. Don't want to overwhelm them."

Larry nodded. Shawna said, "Yeah, we'll stay here, too. You guys get them."

Jack and Jim followed Mr. Walker into the large garage building. There was a big space for cars and an ATV, and stairs going up to a second floor. Mr. Walker led them up the stairs and into a small storage space that was currently occupied by Charlie and the bigfoot family. Charlie was waiting for them and greeted Jim and Jack with shoulder squeezes.

"How are you, Charlie?" Jim asked.

He smiled down at Jim, but it was strained. He was worried that something else would happen. The family stood and came forward. They were ready to get out of here, too.

"Dale, we can't thank you enough for what you did," Jack said. He put out a hand and they shook.

"Dad!"

Eva came running in. She stopped before them, panting with exertion and excitement. She caught Jim's eyes on her and faltered slightly.

"What is it, Eva?" Mr. Walker prompted.

"I didn't want them to leave without me saying bye."

"I wouldn't have let that happen." He patted her on the back.

Eva marched up to Charlie. She stood for a moment, looking unsure of what to do or say.

"Charlie, I'll miss you. It's so great to meet you and know you're out there."

She grabbed his hand and squeezed it, then moved to the left of Charlie and slowly approached Scar.

"You saved me a long time ago, but I've never forgotten. When I saw your scars, I knew it was you. I'm glad I got to meet you and know that you're really good and going to be safe now."

After a second of hesitation and wobbling between moving forward and back, she finally moved forward and gave him a short hug.

Scar's eyes widened and searched for Charlie, who just smiled back at him. Eva broke the hug, and Scar looked down at her with amazement on his face. She then waved to the mother and their babies.

Everyone started moving down the stairs and out to the vehicles. Eva followed behind with Jim. She kept looking at him and opening her mouth to say something, but she never said anything.

As they got to the driveway, Jim turned to her.

"Thanks so much for your help. We couldn't have done it without you guys."

She blushed and smiled.

"I only wish we could have done more. Y'all went through a lot."

"Nah. Nothing we couldn't handle."

She was looking at him, and he couldn't figure out why or what to do next. Finally, she stepped forward and gave him a kiss on the cheek.

"I'll miss you." He felt her slip a piece of paper in his hand. "Here's my email address. Let me know how things are going. With them … and you."

Then her face turned bright red, she blinked rapidly for a moment, then turned and ran to her dad.

Jim was stunned. He felt confused, happy, excited, and sad that they were leaving, all at the same time.

"Dude, way to go. She's cute."

Jim looked over to see Pete watching him with a stupid grin on his face. He felt his face making that same stupid grin right back at him.

Everyone was gathered around the van and RV. The family stood to the side, with Charlie.

Karen looked at Jim and Jack.

"So we have a plan for them," she said, nodding at the bigfoot family.

CHAPTER TWENTY-NINE
The Final Word

THE SOUND OF Shawna's light, pleasant laughter woke Jim. He rolled out of bed and opened the door to his room. Pete's loud guffaw joined in, almost obscuring the sound of Jilly's squeaky giggle.

Curious, Jim stumbled down the stairs. It had been a week since they had left the Walker's home. Karen, Shawna, Pete, and Larry had discussed what to do next while Jim and Jack had been inside getting the family. Their only real option was to drive Scar and his family to the Thomas house and get them situated there. At least for a while. They didn't know if the family would like it or if it really was a big enough space of land for them. For the time being, the safest option was for the bigfoot family to come home with them.

Shawna, Pete, and Larry hadn't wanted just to leave them, so they had stayed and helped with the adjustment. They were staying in the room above the Thomas' spacious garage, and the bigfoot family was camped out in the garage with Charlie. Charlie had moved to the house long ago, but he was helping them adjust there for now. Luckily the garage was very roomy and bright, with plenty of windows, high ceilings, and space for three cars plus extra things, like bikes and ATVs. But it was mostly used for storage, so there was plenty of room for the new hairy family.

Jim got down the stairs and saw what all the laughing was about. Charlie was sitting at the breakfast table in the kitchen, with Jilly standing on the bench behind him. She was braiding his hair and placing bows here and there.

"Oh no. Jilly! I said not to do that anymore!" *Charlie's a guy.*

Shawna laughed. She grabbed Jim's arm as he came into the room and began petting it.

"Aw, Jim. She told us how she used to do this, so we asked her to show us how pretty she can make Charlie look. Calm down, shh. Don't be angry."

Jim laughed. "Aw, shut it. Just don't make him feel too stupid."

Charlie actually looked to be loving the attention. His eyes were closing and relaxed. If he was a cat, Jim thought he would be purring now. Pete had grabbed a brush and began stroking the hair on Charlie's arms. Larry watched the spectacle with a grin.

"Morning," came a voice behind them.

Karen and Jack came into the kitchen and began fixing breakfast. This was the last meal with Shawna, Pete, and Larry. They were going home. Everyone gathered around the table and talked and laughed. It was a great last breakfast together. They had done something amazing together, and the TV crew's lives had changed.

"Hey, so what are you guys going to do now that you know the truth? With your show, I mean," Jack asked.

Shawna looked at Jim.

"Well, Jim and I were talking about that days ago. I'm not sure." She looked at Pete and Larry. "We've been friends for so long, I can't imagine not seeing you guys all the time."

Larry cleared his throat. His eyes began flitting around the room. "I, uh, I have an idea for a movie that I'd like to make. It's kinda based on this stuff. You guys. If you don't mind."

Jack laughed.

"Nothing too close to home."

"Of course not. I'd let you read the script first."

"Well, good luck!"

"Yeah," everyone echoed.

"Would you two like to help?" he asked Shawna and Pete.

"Dude, I'm in!" Pete said.

Shawna nodded with a smile. "Sure. I'll need something to do while I'm waiting to be accepted." She looked around shyly. "I'm thinking about going back to school for some sort of biology degree."

"That's great," Karen encouraged. "You seem to really like science and animals."

"I do. I'd like to be on the forefront of any research into what these guys are. You know, should that day come."

A lull came over the group. They were nearing the end of their time together.

"What about you guys?" Pete asked.

"Hey, yeah. What are you going to do?" Shawna asked.

Jack looked at each of his family members.

"We'll do what we do best now—take care of those of the bigfoot persuasion."

"Yeah, we'll let them live here for as long as they like, but I don't know if they'll stay or need a bigger place to live," Karen added.

"Twenty-one acres should be enough, right?" Pete asked. "Not to mention your neighbor's land. He's never home, and he has, like, a hundred acres."

"This place is amazing," Shawna said. "They should be happy here."

Breakfast ended, and the TV crew left to pack everything up. Jim followed Charlie to the garage. Their long driveway split into a Y, with one side leading to the house and the other leading to the garage. Jim and Charlie walked down one arm of the drive and up the other. It was a hot day, but they were mostly shaded by large trees that were currently full of chirping birds. Jim listened to the sounds of their song and the wind rustling the leaves. Cicadas were attempting to drown out any other sounds, but having spent so many years here, Jim found it to be normal background noise. He was so at peace out here, and he hoped the family would find some peace, too.

Jim pushed the door open and found the family sitting in their little living area. The boy was sitting on a blanket, playing with one of Jim's old Transformers. He was switching it back and forth, absolutely enthralled.

The mother was feeding her baby, and Scar was eating some of the vegetables and fruit Karen had brought. He had supplemented with some things he had found outside with Charlie this morning. Jim hadn't realized all the edible things in their woods, but that didn't mean he was going to start eating acorns or the mussels from the lake anytime soon.

"Hey, how are you?" Jim asked, knowing full well that they wouldn't answer.

Still, Scar gave a friendly wave, and the mother nodded with a smile.

Jim sat down next to the boy and showed him how to fully change the Transformer, much to his delight. He looked around and found an old coloring book the boy had been playing with. His attempts at coloring made Jim laugh, but he couldn't help but think how smart he was to get the Crayons and try.

Charlie sat down next to Scar and began munching some acorns, too. Jim watched their silent comfort.

"Well, Charlie, we didn't find your family, but we found you a family, in a way."

Charlie looked at Jim with a look of contentment. He reached over and began coloring. It was something that had always fascinated him. He liked being able to make colors, and he was actually quite good at drawing.

Jim sighed. He felt like he needed a long vacation after their last one, but he would take just some quiet time at home with his family, Charlie, and the new bigfoot family. They were adjusting well and seemed to like their new home. Jack and Karen were trying to figure out how to keep them all in enough food, since they ate a ton throughout the day. But Karen's new garden that she had started last year was certainly coming in handy.

Watching Charlie, Jim realized that he looked more animated, more confident, and wiser. His movements were more sure, stronger. The new family had made him grow up. Even though it wasn't his family, he was taking charge of them, taking care of them.

He was happy. And that was all that mattered right now.

CPSIA information can be obtained
at www.ICGtesting.com
Printed in the USA
FFHW020018110219
50490232-55734FF

9 781941 536629